The BATTLE of the SUN

JEANETTE WINTERSON

BLOOMSBURY

LONDON BERLIN NEW YORK

Bloomsbury Publishing, London, Berlin and New York

First published in Great Britain in 2009 by Bloomsbury Publishing Plc
36 Soho Square, London, W1D 3QY

A CIP catalogue record of this book is available from the British Library

Hardback ISBN 978 1 4088 0042 3
Export ISBN 978 1 4088 0150 5

All papers used by Bloomsbury Publishing are natural, recyclable products made
from wood grown in well-managed forests. The manufacturing processes conform
to the environmental regulations of the country of origin.

Typeset by Dorchester Typesetting Group Ltd
Printed in the United States of America by Worldcolor Fairfield

3 5 7 9 10 8 6 4

www.bloomsbury.com

To my godchildren,
Eleanor and Cara Shearer,
who made this happen,
and to myself, a long time ago.
Woof!

CONTENTS

On the fourteenth of August 1601, the Keeper of the Tides
dropped his net into the River Thames,
and pulled out a golden fish.

THE CLOCK STRIKES TWELVE

It began as all important things begin – by chance. It was about twelve o'clock midday. The Thames was busy with boats of every kind; oarboats, sailboats, whelk boats, wherries, tideboats, oyster boats, barges, boats scooped out simple as a saucer – flat and shallow and so small that a cat could ride in one by himself. Great boats gilded, decked, cushioned, studded, crimsoned, velveted, proud, pennants and flags flying. Dragboats towing trees for timber, fishing boats, where a boy leant against the mast, arms waving, out over the waves and slop of the tidal river.

The water-craft came from every side, and down the middle too, so that there was no upriver and downriver, only a stream of boats, a race of boats, hugger-mugger, dodging one another, grazing one another, sometimes so close that a man putting a sausage to his mouth found he had fed the lady at the oars in the whelk boat next to him.

The sun was on the river so that everything seemed brighter and more lit up that day. Even the severed heads of the traitors, pitched on their tall spikes at Temple Bar, had the look of pompom bushes waiting to come into leaf. Jack thought he saw one of the heads look straight at him, but it must have been the sun in his eyes.

Jack. He heard the clock strike midday. To tell the truth Jack was chiming twelve himself, like the clock at midday. It was his birthday and he was twelve years old on the fourteenth of August. He counted the clock, nine, ten, eleven, twelve. Twelve years old in the Year of Our Lord 1601.

Jack ran, pushing and zigging and zagging through the sellers and hawkers on the riverbank. He was tall for his age, and his mother had apprenticed him early to a printer and bookbinder. He would live with half a dozen other boys, and serve his master for seven years. But all that would start tomorrow, and first he was going to be given a spaniel for his birthday. He knew the spaniel, he had seen the spaniel, he had named the spaniel. Max. Max Max Max! The best of a litter of four pups, and Jack's very own dog.

Jack's mind that day was all spaniel, there was nothing in it but spaniel. There were no thoughts of food or drink or school or a ball blown out of a pig's bladder and kicked halfway across London with his friends. Inside Jack's head was a night-sky-black dog with stars that were his eyes, and ears soft as sleep. Jack was so almost a spaniel himself that day that he nearly ran four-legged the faster to get home.

Home was the big house that sat between the Strand and the River Thames. It was known to everyone as The Level, though no one seemed to know why, and it belonged to Sir Roger Rover, a man with green eyes and a red beard, who some said was a pirate, but if he was a pirate he was a very good pirate, for the Queen herself was fond of him, and often sent him off to sea on her private business.

In this house, Jack's mother Anne lived as housekeeper, and Jack did jobs around the stable-yard, fetching water, polishing tack, sweeping the courtyards for the many visitors who clattered through the great arch off the Strand.

It was a fine house, a fair house, whose gardens let on to the river itself, and it was to the water-gate, and through those gardens, that Jack was coming home, when . . . When . . . it happened.

Two men, short, hooded, black boots, black cloaks, black hats, were waiting either side of the water-gate. As Jack came through, panting from his run, the men seized his body, pinioned his arms, threw a rough damp torn sack over him and bundled him into a waiting boat.

'Be this the one?'

'This be the one, sure as I have a tongue and one ear.'

His accomplice laughed. 'If he be not the one, you shall have a tongue or one ear but never both on the same head.'

'Quiet, you water-rat! Give him the drink.'

The man held back Jack's head and opened his mouth with his fingers, as you would to a dog, then the other fellow poured a thick red liquid down Jack's throat. Jack spat and coughed and choked, but he had to swallow some of it. It tasted bitter. It was gritty. It was like fire ashes or fine-ground oyster shells mixed up in red vinegar.

The men shoved Jack into a closed coop at the stern of the boat. It was a poultry boat and there was a big slatted wooden hen-coop perched at one end where the fowls were rowed to market. Jack looked out through the torn sack and the slats of the boat; the boat was being rowed rapidly east. Jack wanted to shout out, but he couldn't because he was dizzy, and the last thing he saw were the boats on the river no longer going up and down, but round and round and round and round like at a fair.

Jack felt a great dullness, like the world spinning to a stop at the end of time. He passed into a dead and dreamless sleep, a black place.

The men in the boat sat still without speaking. One lit a clay pipe.

As the boat reached its mooring place, several servants dressed in grey came to meet it. Jack was carried from the coop, and the boat and the two men rowed on, distant now, towards Limehouse.

The servants took Jack down and down and down. They laid him there and walked away. There was nothing more to do.

At home, his small spaniel could not be quieted, and ran up and down, down and up, stopping and crying in a dark corner of the room. Jack's mother, standing at the water-gate, had a sense, an instinct, that her son was alive but in danger.

'He is a boy, he's fallen over, he's eating apples, he's met with a friend,' said the groom, wondering why women never used good commonsense but fretted and worried over simple foolish things.

'He was to be here at twelve midday,' said Jack's mother, 'and if he comes not to be here by twelve at midnight, then shall I go to him.'

'And how shall that be done?' said the groom, laughing at her, 'in all the teeming city of London, its lanes, lodgings, highways and byways, inns and dens, how shall you, a woman, find one strayed boy?'

But Jack's mother knew how she would find her son. She went up to her room and opened the little door in the wall, and took out a small leather bag with something inside.

THE FISH WITHOUT FINS

J ack woke up.

It was dark.

But what was the 'it' that was dark?

Jack felt like he was inside a giant animal, and he remembered the Bible story of Jonah and the whale, and he wondered if, on the river, the boat had sunk and he had been swallowed by a great fish?

The darkness was so dark that when Jack put his hand to his nose, he could feel his nose but he couldn't see his hand.

He lay still. He tried to remember exactly what had happened. Two men . . . the boat . . .

Jack felt underneath under him; he seemed to be on a floor of hard smooth stone. He listened carefully; it was dull and muffled like somebody whispering. He could hear water. He had no idea what the inside of a whale was like, but it might be like this. If it was a room of some kind it must have walls, and Jack couldn't find any walls, not even now that he was crawling, blind, hoping to find something that he knew from another life. It felt like another life; everything up to this moment of opening his eyes in the black place felt like another life. His mother – she would worry. His spaniel, his new spaniel that he had seen in a heap of sacks with three brothers and sisters, and been promised for today. Or was it today? How much time had passed?

As Jack crawled, his head straight in front like a dog's, he brushed against something rough and swinging. He felt it; it was a rope. Jack pulled, first cautiously, then with all his strength, like ringing the great bell in church. The rope held. Jack used it to pull himself upright. Then, making sure of the ground under his feet in case he fell, Jack swung his whole weight on to the rope, hanging just above ground. The rope held.

'I'll climb it,' said Jack, out loud.

He was a good climber, strong and lithe, and up he went, hand over hand, his feet cupping together and pushing off the rope below. He climbed and climbed, and if he was tired, he did not notice it. What he did notice was that the rope was now wet. Not damp. Soaking wet. Then he realised that he himself was wet. Not damp. Soaking wet. He was climbing through water, which was impossible because he was breathing quite normally. It was as though he was a fish in its own element. *Have I become a fish?* thought Jack. *Have I been swallowed by a fish and made into a fish myself?*

Then Jack understood something that frightened him very much; as a boy, he was climbing a rope, vertically. As a fish, he was being pulled on a rope, horizontally, through the water. If he was a boy, he was climbing. If he was a fish, this rope was a line, and he was caught.

There was a sudden tug above him, and he was no longer climbing, but holding on, as his body surged upwards

14

through the water, water streaming off him as though he had gills and fins, his hair that had been tied back now loose and flowing like the water-fish he was.

Without warning, Jack came flying over the broad stone rim of a well, gasping for air, flat on his face on the cobbles of a courtyard. He lay panting – his mouth opening and closing. He could see a pair of well-polished leather riding boots and two pairs of cloth shoes.

'Good day, my young Fish,' said a voice, and then, 'Young gentlemen! At last you see before you the beginning of the Opus. Certainly this is the one we were seeking. Here is the Fish without Fins!'

Jack raised his head. He tried to stand up but slipped in his own pool of water. The man clapped his hands. 'William! Robert!' Two boys, near his own age, bent down and helped Jack to his feet. He brushed himself off, shaking the water from his hair and wiping his eyes. The back of his hand crossed his forehead, and when he took his hand away he saw it was glistening with scales. He rubbed at them with his other hand, and they fell away, leaving his skin clear and smooth, as it usually was.

The man standing before him looked amused, and gave Jack his handkerchief to dry his face. Jack wiped his face and neck and stuffed the handkerchief into his sodden jacket pocket. The man spoke.

'Welcome, Adam Kadmon.'

'I am not Adam,' said Jack. 'My name is Jack Snap.'

'Nevertheless, your name is Adam.'

The man who spoke was tall, dark, bearded, of an age hard to describe, not young, not old, richly dressed, his fingers each with a gold ring. The man made a sign, and a servant wrapped Jack in a grey blanket. Jack pulled it round him, shivering, and looked back at the well.

It was a well, an ordinary courtyard well, but without a bucket or a pulley. The rope that had pulled him out was coiled around a device such as ships use for hauling the anchor. The well was in a courtyard surrounded by high stone walls. There was only one door to the outside.

'There is no way out,' said the man, reading Jack's thoughts, 'at least not such a way as you seek. You will be set free when your work is done, but it cannot be done before you begin.'

'I am to be an apprentice to a printer and bookbinder,' said Jack, 'and my mother is at home waiting for me. Let me go.'

The man laughed. 'I came across the sea to find you. I travelled through foreign lands to find you. I cannot let you go quite so soon, my fishboy.'

'There was no water at the bottom of the well,' said Jack, 'and yet there was water at the top of the well. How can that be?'

'It was no common water in the well,' answered the man. 'Things here are not as they seem elsewhere.'

'What is this place?' asked Jack, looking up to the lead roof of the building. The house was like a church but not a church. It seemed to be made of stone and lead, which was strange in a city made mostly of wood; its houses wood, its shops and markets, bridges and wharves, theatres and taverns, all wood. London was a wooden city, like a forest remade for people to live in, and sometimes, a house sprouted leaves, where the green oak was still alive. But this house did not feel like a house where anything had ever been alive.

'This is the Dark House,' said the man. 'Come inside . . .'

THE DARK HOUSE

There never was such a house. Jack passed through an ill-lit hall into a long wide room lined with books. He had never seen so many books, each in its leather binding, most of them with their titles in Latin or a different alphabet, which he guessed must be Greek. Jack had learned some Latin at school, like the other boys, and he could read and write English, but he knew nothing of Greek, though his mother had said he would have to learn his letters for the printing press.

The books sat on wide stone shelves. The long stone-mullioned windows had no curtains, and the stone walls of the room had no tapestries or hangings. In the centre of the room was a circular stone table that looked part like an altar in church, and part like a sundial in the garden.

'A clever observation,' said the man, and Jack was startled, because the man had read his mind.

There were a few chairs in the room, and each chair was carved out of a massy single stone, the seat scooped out in a curve as though a giant had taken a spoon to a block of snow.

The floor was stone, the fireplace was stone, though no fire burned there, and although it was midsummer the room was cold. No sun fell through the long windows, which was strange, because outside the light was radiant. It was as though the sun himself avoided the Dark House.

Without speaking, the man led Jack back into the hall and up the wide stone staircase, broad and austere. Up they went, past closed rooms and along empty passages, the walls bare, the air itself bare. Jack felt like he was breathing emptiness.

At the end of a long corridor was an opening without doors. The man stood inside and let Jack go in first. This room was a dormitory. There were seven stone beds in a line, and six of them had been occupied that morning, for on each of the six stone beds was a straw-stuffed mattress, a straw-stuffed pillow, and a pair of coarse grey horse blankets. The window in the room gave on to the courtyard, and down below Jack could see the servants in their grey livery. He was interested to see that they had brought out a small coach and were backing two grey geldings into the traces.

'Yes, I have an appointment,' said the man, 'but there are others who will watch over you until my return. You will sleep here.'

'I don't want to sleep here,' said Jack.

'Then you shall not sleep at all,' said the man. 'When you are tired enough, you shall sleep here.'

'What do you want of me?' said Jack. 'You have many servants.'

'I am in want of a servant of a very particular kind,' said the man, 'and you are that particular kind.'

The man turned and left the room, walking rapidly down

the passageway. Jack felt a pull, like metal to a magnet, and he followed the man, although he did not want to.

There's some magic here, he thought, and he was afraid. He noticed the man's split-second pause, and knew that he had read his mind again. Jack's next thought wasn't a thought at all, but he determined in his heart that if there was magic here he would find it out, know its power, and make his escape.

In the library the man was standing with a metal key by a metal wall with a metal door. 'This is where we strive for the Opus,' he said.

Jack knew that 'opus' was Latin for 'work', but he didn't know what he would see on the other side of the door.

As the heavy door swung slowly open, Jack felt a great heat scorch his face. He saw a fire burning under a glass bottle so big that a horse could have used it as a stall. The glass bottle had a wide fat base where the flames heated it, and then it shaped itself into a sphere before narrowing into a funnel. Steam, green, blue and red, issued from the funnel.

The room was all colour, in strange contrast to the grey bare and empty house. The walls were painted deep red and had numbers and signs marked on them. The floor was blue, and on it, painted in gold, were two triangles upside down to each other, forming a star. Jack knew what this was; it was a pentangle. He had seen such signs and symbols before because his mother had once been housekeeper to the great alchemist, John Dee.

'John Dee . . .' said the man, reading Jack's thoughts as Jack became nervous.

'He is the Queen's own alchemist!' said Jack, noticing how the man frowned angrily. Jack looked away. The man was frightening when he was angry.

The room was stacked with jars of all sizes and shapes. Some of the jars held animals preserved in fluid. There was a fox upright, its nose bobbing against the seal. There was a carp with a gold ring in its mouth. Some jars contained volatile liquids that hissed and pressed against the glass as though they would escape. Other jars were filled with coloured stones, others with seaweed, others with earth. There were salts and dyes and vinegars and acids. There were jars cloudy with their own steam, and jars that shone silver like the polished inside of a pearl oyster.

As Jack walked among the shelves he saw a long jar with a leg in it, and a shorter jar with an arm in it, and a square jar with two hands in it, and a jar like a fishbowl with a head in it.

On a pedestal was a head made out of bronze, but lifelike and fine. The smallest boy that Jack had ever seen was sitting beside the head. The boy's own head was covered in bright red curly hair, and because it stood on end it made him look like he had a perpetual fright. He was nearly nodding asleep, his thin legs locked around the legs of the stool, and he looked as though he had been sitting there for ever.

'He is waiting for the Head to speak,' said the man, 'as surely it will one day if my calculations are right.'

Two other boys were pumping air into the furnace, wielding giant bellows about six feet long. A fourth boy was perched at the top of a wooden ladder, pouring green liquid through an opening in the funnel of the vessel.

'That vessel is called a retort,' said the man.

'It is called a retort, though some call it an alembic,' said Jack.

'Very good,' said the man. 'Yes, this great jar is the retort or the alembic, and from its mysteries will come such marvels as will change the world for ever.'

Jack was not sure that he wanted the world to change – not even for a day and a night, let alone for ever. He loved to wake up in the mornings, early, and find the sun crossing the floor of his little room, and go down to the river as the day was beginning, and catch a fish, or run, just because he was happy, then begin his jobs with the horses and their soft breath and strong animal smell. Every day was different enough to be interesting and the same enough to be safe. He did not see why the world had to change, unless it was to make a small opening to let in the small black body of a small black spaniel.

'To open the world – even to let in a dog – is to change it for ever,' said the man. 'You do not understand that, but you will, if you are what I believe you are.'

'What am I?' said Jack.

But the man did not answer. His servant was at the door.

'I will return very soon. The others will tell you what we do here – Robert! William!'

The two boys whom Jack had sighted in the courtyard, the

ones who had helped him to his feet, came running over from where they had been sorting materials at the back of the laboratory. Robert was a good-looking, dark-haired boy of about twelve or thirteen. William was blond and light with a watchful darting face like a monkey.

'You will tell Jack of our Work here,' said the man, and the two boys nodded, looking curiously at Jack.

'If you won't tell me what I am,' said Jack, 'will you tell me who you are?'

The man bowed a short sharp bow, and smiled his smile that was not a smile. 'I am the Magus. That is all you need to know.'

The Magus left the room, and in a second Jack heard the jilting sound of the carriage wheels and the iron clatter of the horses' hooves across the cobbles in the courtyard.

The boys heard it too, and the others stopped their work to gather around Jack. Robert seemed to be the leader, with William as his Second. Robert introduced Jack to the other boys.

There was Peter, who was small and round and red in the face from his bellows work. He looked like a heated pudding. There was Anselm, who was thin and thoughtful. He smiled at Jack shyly. There was Roderick, who had worked the bellows with Peter, and who had a cheerful face and black hair poking out from under a red cap. And there was the tiny child with red curly hair, creeping in last and hiding behind Robert's legs.

Robert spoke. 'Are you an orphan, Jack?'

'I have no father, but I have a mother.'

'She abandoned you, did she?'

'No!'

'Then what are you doing here, Jack? This is an orphan place. All of us that you see here come without mother or father. That is what enables us to do the Work.'

'What kind of work is it that you must do without mother or father?'

Robert signalled to Peter, who went across the room and dragged a lead bucket over to Jack. The bucket was filled with small pieces of lead – lead nails, lead shot, short lengths of lead piping, lead caps for gutters. The bucket and its contents were so heavy that the boy could hardly move it.

The tiny child piped up, 'We have to turn all this into gold.'

'Lead into gold?' said Jack, who was pretending to know less than he did know.

'Yes, and every bit of it. If we could do it, it would be easy, but we can't do it, and so it is impossible.'

'What's your name?' said Jack to the child, and the child answered, 'Crispis.'

'That means "curly hair" in Latin,' said Anselm. 'I hope you can read Latin well, Jack. You'll be beaten if you can't.'

'Why do I have to read Latin?' asked Jack.

'The magic books are all in Latin,' said Roderick.

'Is it spells you are casting?' asked Jack.

'If you call the Magus a magician he will beat you for that too,' said Robert. 'He is a Master, he is the Magus.'

27

'He's going to turn all the city of London into gold!' said Crispis.

'But he can't,' said Anselm. 'He can't even turn a horse-shoe into gold – see!'

Anselm pointed to the corner of the room, where there was a heap of horseshoes.

Jack started to walk around, trying to understand everything. At the back of the laboratory was a smaller glass alembic swirling with vapour. As Jack looked at it closely, the vapour cleared and a pair of eyes darted a malevolent look at him. Jack stepped back, frightened.

'What's in there?' he asked.

'That's the Eyebat,' said William. 'Don't like it, do you?' And Jack thought that it was William he didn't like. William started tapping on the glass.

'Stop that!' said Robert.

'Why should I?' demanded William. 'Two nasty mean little eyes that fly about, and nothing else.' William's own eyes were mean and nasty, Jack thought, but he said nothing.

'The Magus is trying to make an homunculus – do you know what that is?' asked Peter, his round red face sweating. Jack shook his head.

'Look at all the bottles! The arms and legs! He wants to join them up and make a little man – an homunculus, which will do his bidding,' said Anselm.

'But he can't!' shouted Crispis. 'Ha ha!'

The boys all looked round in fear and Crispis clapped his hand over his mouth. The leg in the test tube gave a violent kick.

28

'A long time ago the Magus made a Creature in a bottle,' said Robert. 'He had a special assistant at that time, before any of us were here, and the assistant gave him powers he has never had since.'

'What happened to the assistant?' asked Jack, not liking the sound of this, as it might be a warning to himself.

'He disappeared,' said Roderick.

'No one knows,' said Peter.

'He grew up,' said Anselm.

'He was killed! Murdered! Dead!' shouted Crispis. William went over to the elf-sized child and picked him up and hung him by his jacket on a hook.

'You don't know, none of you knows anything!' shouted William.

'That's enough!' said Robert.

The boys stood, tense and silent. To break the moment Jack went over to the Eyebat's jar and tapped the glass. The horrible eyes flew forward and glared at him.

'Please stop it!' said Peter. 'And never open the lid!'

Jack didn't think he ever would take the lid off. He didn't like the thought of those nasty eyes flying around the room like a bat that wasn't blind. He went and sat by the bucket of lead, playing with the shot through his fingers.

'Why don't we escape?' said Jack. 'We could escape now and go to where my mother lives.'

Robert looked sad. 'This is the Dark House and there is no escape.'

There was a terrible noise like an avalanche. It was an

avalanche. Half a forest of wood suddenly fell down a chute into the room. The boys jumped up.

'To the fires!' said Robert. And as the boys turned towards their work with the timber to stoke the fires, Jack went over and lifted Crispis down from the hook. Then he went to help the others.

'Get to work, Crispis!' snapped William.

Crispis tried to pick up a big bit of wood and fell over, pinned underneath and squirming like a kitten.

'Leave him be!' said William. 'Every boy must perform his own tasks. That is the Rule.'

Jack didn't answer. He freed Crispis, and took up a saw beside him. William scowled and looked to Robert to back him up but Robert pretended not to see.

Crispis said, 'Thank you, Jack.' Then he said, 'I wish I were a mouse that lived on peas.'

'He says things like that,' said Robert, tapping his head to show that Crispis of the bright and red and curly hair might have peas for brains.

But Jack was busy with his own thoughts. His mind was working feverishly, thinking of how to escape while the Magus was away.

There was a grating noise, and Jack looked round to see that the metal door in the metal wall had opened and the strangest creature in the world was coming in. He was a man; that is, he was a woman . . . that is, he was a man and a woman, that is, he was . . . he was . . . WHAT . . . ? ?

THE CREATURE SAWN
IN TWO

The Creature who came into the room was cleaved in half straight down the middle, so that one half of it had one eye and one eyebrow, one nostril, one ear, one arm, one leg, one foot, and the other half had just the same.

Well, nearly just the same, because as if the Creature did not astonish enough, one half of it was male and the other half of it was female. The female half had a bosom, or certainly half a bosom.

The Creature appeared to be made of flesh, like a human being, but what human being born is cleaved in half?

The Creature's clothes were as odd as the Creature itself.

The male half wore a shirt with one sleeve, and a pair of breeches with one leg, and where the other sleeve and other leg should have been, was a cut-off and sewn-up side. The Creature had a sleeveless leather jerkin over his shirt, and his jerkin had not been altered in any way, so it looked as though half of it was unfilled with body, which was true.

Beneath the breeches, or perhaps the breech, as the garment must be called, having one leg and not two, was a stocking fastened at the knee, and a stout leather shoe on the bottom of the stocking.

The Creature had no beard, but wore in his single ear a single gold earring.

Its other half was just as bizarre. This lady wore half a skirt, half a chemise and half a hat on her half of the head.

At her waist, or that portion of herself which would have been a waist, dangled a great bunch of keys. She wore no earring, but her hand, more slender than the other, had a ring on each finger.

The expression on either half of the face was disagreeable.

'Seven water rats came out of a drain,' said the Male.

'And none of 'em went back in again . . . ha ha ha!' said the Female.

'They must work harder!' said the Male.

'Or nothing from the larder!' said the Female.

The Creature then hopped swiftly into the room, and instead of standing as one, divided itself into its two halves, each half hopping madly around the room in opposite directions, and beating the boys over the head. Jack hid himself behind the alembic, but he was soon discovered.

'The Seventh is the one to watch!'

'Master's new catch!'

And the two stood balefully in front of Jack, swaying slightly to keep their balance.

'What are you?' said Jack.

'He wants to know What Are You!' said the Female, laughing, and as she laughed, Jack saw she had but one tooth in her head.

'The Creature Sawn in Two!' said the Male. 'Yes we are, yes we are, yes we are.'

'Who sawed you in two?' asked Jack.

'Master, that's who. Made us in a jar then split us like we are.'

'What's your mother and father, then?' asked Jack.

'Ha, mother's a bottle and father's a fire,' said the Female.

'Like breeds like, desire breeds desire,' said the Male.

Jack wondered what they were talking about, but he was only asking questions because he was so scared that he wanted time to steady himself so that he would know what to do next. The metal door was open, and he was half thinking of making a run for it. His eyes must have given him away, for in an instant, the Female was hopping off to close it with a clang, while the Male said, 'Half a thought is worse than none.'

And the Female answered, 'Least said, less done.'

Jack's heart clanged shut like the door, but he found courage, and said, 'Have you names?'

'My name is Wedge. She who you see is Mistress Split.'

'That's it!' cried she.

They smiled – that is, each end of their half-mouth rose towards each ear, like someone reaching for an apple on a branch too far away.

'Pleased to meet you, Jackster, I'm sure I'm not,' said Mistress Split.

'Another silly boy locked away and forgot,' said Wedge. 'You won't get away, not if you try all your life.'

'And if you try, there's always the knife!' said Mistress Split, pulling from the folds of her skirt, where her other leg should have been, a knife the length of a sword. 'There's advantages to a one-legged being.'

Suddenly Wedge grabbed Jack by the neck and with powerful strength forced him to his knees.

'But what advantage to a no-headed being? Eh, Jackster?'

With a laugh and a push Wedge threw Jack on to the floor. Mistress Split kicked him, and with a gasp and an ouch Jack saw that her shoe had an iron toe and an iron heel. He didn't move.

The Creature(s) hopped away, yelling at the boys, and laughing their high maniacal laugh; then, as Jack stayed where he was, he heard the metal door open and shut, followed by the hopping noise of what he would come to learn as the iron shoe.

As soon as the Creature(s) had gone, Robert came over to Jack and helped him on to a barrel and gave him water to drink. Anselm fetched him a piece of bread and cheese. Jack realised he was starving.

'Beware of them, Jack,' said Robert. 'They have no pity and great strength. The Magus made them before we came here.'

'Yes,' said Anselm. 'He made them and they were one, like we are one, but they tried to disobey him and as a punishment he tore them in two. Now they are full of fear of him and hate of everyone.'

'They will never show you any mercy or any kindness, none,' said Robert.

36

'When he made them, were they at once a male and a female?' asked Jack, finishing his bread.

'Yes, it was a great wonder,' said Peter.

'What is their purpose?'

'To spy on us, and to keep us here. They know everything,' said Robert.

'What of the other servants? The ones in grey?'

'All too afraid. They do not speak to us.'

'We will escape,' said Jack. 'I promise you I will find a way.'

Robert shook his head sadly. 'Before you came, we were seven, and the seventh tried to escape.'

'What became of him?'

Robert stood up from the barrel and gestured at Jack to follow. He went towards the back of the laboratory and opened a door. The room beyond was very dark, except for a row of candles which seemed to be burning in front of some statues.

'Are these statues from the Catholic churches or the monasteries?' asked Jack, who knew that King Henry the Eighth, the king before Elizabeth had become queen, had made England a Protestant country and had all the statues taken out of all the Catholic churches. Some people had taken the statues and hidden them in their houses, some because they continued in secret to be Catholics, and some because they were sorry to see the old and colourful ways disappear, with their statues of saints and virgins. They were, after all, someone to talk to, and many an ordinary wife missed her quiet talks with a statue that she would swear seemed to speak.

Robert shook his head. 'They are the ones who Disobeyed.'

'Hear what he says?' said William. 'DISOBEYED!'

Jack ignored his stare, and went closer to look at the statues.

They were life-size, and life-like. Only a master carver could have made anything so like a human being.

'They were human beings,' said Robert.

And Jack noticed the sad expressions on their faces – very sad and very surprised. Two had their mouths a little open, as though they had been about to speak.

A boy, very like Jack in height and build, stood silent and upright at the end of the row. Jack put out his hand and touched the boy's face. Yes, the boy was stone. Stone-hard and stone-cold. No sun could warm him now.

'We light the candles here,' said Peter, 'so that they are not always in the dark.'

'Are they alive inside the stone?' said Jack. 'Or are they all stone?'

'No one can tell,' said Robert. 'And their lips are stone, so they cannot tell.'

Jack ran his finger over the boy's lips, and felt something like infinite sadness, but whether it was his own sadness, or that of the stone boy, he could not tell.

Back inside the laboratory, the boys finished sawing and

stacking the wood. They built up the furnace and drained and filled the liquids. They seemed cheerful at their work, for, as Robert explained, the laboratory was the only place in the Dark House that was warm, and it was the only place that was not grey. Here in the colour and warmth, and the light flowing down from the windows set in the roof, the boys were as free and as happy as they could be. There was water too, so they were not thirsty, and they were fed bread and cheese at noon and bread and broth at four o'clock, and they ate it sitting by the furnace, talking and joking and playing games. They hated the dark dormitory, and the silent fearful seven o'clock breakfasts, after the long tramp down and down the stairs, Wedge in front, Mistress Split behind. At seven every evening they were summoned for supper, the Magus sweeping through the refectory like a dark wind.

It was evening, and growing dark outside. Wedge came hopping in to the laboratory and herded the boys to their stations in the long refectory. There was a large round loaf on the table, and a cooked leg of mutton. Mistress Split pulled her sword from her skirt and brought it down, SLICE! WHOOSH! SLICE! WHOOSH! Mutton and bread flew in the air and landed about the table, while the boys fetched their pieces and ate it, all the while listening to the mad rhymes and manic laughter of the Creature(s).

'What rhymes with Loaf?'

'Oaf!'

'What rhymes with Mutton?'

'Glutton!'

The two sat at the head of the table, so close together that they were nearly one. Each ate noisily, snatching food from the other, and cramming it into their half-mouths. Jack had once seen a snake with two heads that could only feed and not starve if one head was distracted by a twig or a nail while the other head ate. If not both heads spat and snarled so much that neither could swallow.

And Jack thought that perhaps the way to defeat these two that were one that were two, was to turn them against each other.

As he thought this the Magus entered the room, and Jack forced himself not to think at all.

At the end of the meal the boys were marched upstairs and locked into the stone room with the stone beds. The moon herself, usually so soft and kind, seemed made of stone that night, her light hard and held.

One by one the boys fell asleep, but Jack did not fall asleep. He lay awake, thinking of his mother and his little black dog, and he thought he heard, far off, his dog barking.

Somehow he would get away.

MOTHER MIDNIGHT

It was five minutes to the hour. Jack's mother rose from her chair by the window and, taking the little leather bag, wrapped her cloak around her shoulders and quietly slipped out of the house and down on to the river.

The night was misty and cool. A swan white as a ghost glided by, silent as a ghost, and like a ghost, without visible means of movement.

Jack's mother shivered in the air and hurried on. She knew where she was going.

As she made her way to London Bridge, it seemed as though the whole city was whispering to her. The wooden and plaster houses echoed and reverberated any noise, and the noise of the Thames and its water-wheels and conduits was like a giant whisper that jumped from house to house.

TSHSH, TSHSH, TSHSH. Jack's mother listened, and behind the whispering she heard a horse's hooves, far off, and the sound of a pail being emptied from an upper room.

At the bridge her old friend the Keeper of the Tides was leaning out of his poop-window that overlooked the river.

It was late, and he had to open the bridge gate to let her cross.

'What news,' he called to her, 'that you are out so late?'

'My Jack is missing!' she said.

'This is a strange time!' he answered. 'The river rises too high, the moon sinks too low. Something is going to happen!'

'So I fear,' said Anne, 'but I must hurry on.'

She crossed London Bridge, and disappeared into a maze of narrow alleys around Southwark. There, all noise ended. She was in a silence as thick as cloth.

She walked, hearing nothing but her own footsteps, until she came to a small door with the sign of a pentangle above it on the lintel. She knocked three times.

After a few moments the door opened, and there in the shadows of the doorway stood an old woman with eyes like diamonds. There was a black cat draped across her shoulders, and the cat had eyes like red rubies.

What a figure the woman was – so small she could have lived in a box. So thin that she could have escaped from a hole in a box. Her mouth was as empty as an empty box, and her eyes were as full of secrets as a box that says DO NOT OPEN. She was not a human, not a fish, not a cat, not a dog, not a monster, not a devil, not a born thing, not anything. She was all manner of things. She was Mother Midnight.

Mother Midnight's house was not like a house – it was like a den round the foot of a tree. Past the door there was a narrow passage that led to a room whose ceiling was so low that Jack's mother had to stoop until she could sit down. There were no windows, and the walls were hung with sacking to keep the wind out. A fire roared in the chimney – a fire of such a size that it lit the room without any further light, and heated the room like an oven. And yet there was not a stick of wood to be seen, and the fire had a red look to it, like the eyes of the cat. A kettle and a cauldron hung to the side of the fire.

In the centre of the room was an oak tree of vast girth, whose lower branches seemed to form the roof or ceiling of Mother Midnight's den. The roots of the tree were in the ground and the tree was alive. Planks of wood had been fitted round the tree to form a table, and there were several chairs carved from fallen oak around this table. On the table was a shallow copper bowl filled with green water.

There was nothing else in the room but a straw mattress and a broom.

Jack's mother wasted no time. She told of what had happened that day, and how Jack had not come home these twelve hours gone, and of her fears that Jack had been kidnapped.

Mother Midnight sat down, and passed her hands over the copper bowl. She seemed to fall into a kind of trance as the green water clouded over and swirled and steamed with strange colours and mists.

Then, like a vision in the water, was Jack's face. His mother cried out, putting her hand to her mouth. She could see the stone bed and the stone window and the moon like a pale stone outside. And there was her beloved boy.

'He is not harmed,' said Mother Midnight.

'Who has taken him?'

'That I cannot tell you, for I am forbidden by a power stronger than mine own.'

'Then the danger is great!'

'His spirit is strong and clear,' said Mother Midnight. 'I can feel him strong and clear.'

'Where is he?'

'You must search for him and find him yourself.'

'I have the magnet.'

Jack's mother took the magnet out of its leather bag, and she had a glove belonging to Jack. She passed them over to Mother Midnight, who sat muttering over them and turning them in her old scarred hands.

'Now it is charged,' she said. 'Now the magnet will be drawn to the boy as if to metal.'

'Is it witchcraft that has him?' asked Jack's mother.

'It is a dark power,' said Mother Midnight, 'and more you shall not know until more you shall know.'

The fire hissed and spat like a cat. The water in the bowl settled and became still and green once more.

Jack's mother stood up, stooping under the ceiling of mud and branches, and leaving money on the table, she left without speaking. The magnet had a heat to it now, and she felt it pulling her towards Lambeth.

She didn't notice a very small black dog following her.

THE SUNKEN KING

I n the dead of night Jack woke up. The light of the moon was shining directly on his face and across the floor towards the door. Jack swung out of bed and pulled on his jacket and shoes.

He tried the door. It was locked, but Jack knew what to do. His own father had been a master blacksmith, and before he died he had given Jack an iron tool with blades and picks and pokes and prongs that were all folded together, as many as you could count. The bit of iron didn't look like much unless you opened it out – it looked like something for picking stones out of horses' hooves, or paring your nails, or gouging a hole in a block of wood, but that was a good thing because it meant that no one wanted to steal it.

Very quietly Jack jigged the iron tool in the lock. There was a sharp click and the door opened. In a second Jack was out of the room and down the stone stairs.

At the third turn of the stairs, Jack saw a door half open, and the low light of a lantern burning. There was a noise. Jack hesitated, poised as a cat, and crept along the wall. He could see no shadow moving on the floor of the room, so he guessed that someone was sleeping in there. Jack took a deep breath, held his breath, and crossed the opening of the door.

He could not help glancing inside, and what he saw stopped him in astonishment.

It was the room of the Creature(s).

A bed was sawn in two, and each lay snoring in his and her own half. Each had half a pillow, with the straw stuffing falling out, and half a blanket with the threads unravelling. By each half a bed was half a table and on each half a table burned half a tallow candle.

By the window was a chair split down the middle, and over the back of one half of the chair were his clothes, and over the back of the other half of the chair were her clothes. On the wall was a painting of a green lion, but the painting had been roughly broken in two, and the jagged edges of the canvas pointed at each other. Jack looked down at the floorboards underneath the painting. It was a strange thing – it was as if the painting had just been painted and the halved lion was leaking gold. There were little gold spatters, like candle wax, all over the floor.

Jack was hypnotised by the room. The breathing of the Creature(s) was like a spell. He felt himself being drawn in, closer and closer to the bed, to the half-body, to the half-face. He put out his hand.

Suddenly he seemed to hear a little dog bark, and he came to his senses, and shook himself, like a dog that has fallen into the water and jumps out.

Boldly, he snatched up the candle from the table nearest to the door, and made his way again down the dark stairs towards the hall, where he was sure he could unlock the front door and find his way home.

But as he reached the hallway, he heard an unmistakable sound of groaning and a voice, wavering and thin, that cried, 'Help me! Help me!'

Jack hesitated. The door to the courtyard was right in front of him. He had his iron tool. He could escape. *Now, now, now.* And the voice came again, 'Help me! Help me!'

Jack turned. He moved quickly towards the back of the hallway, and saw steps going down, down. It was pitch black, so black that his candle only lit the tiny square around his feet. Cautiously he took the steps one by one, as they became damper, danker, and he wondered if this was the way into the well.

There was no sound. 'Who's there?' called Jack.

The groaning began again. It was behind him. Jack turned and saw a tiny opening in the wall, very low, so that he had to stoop to get in. As he bent under the mossy lintel, and straightened himself up again, he saw an unlit torch on the wall, and he lit it with his candle. The torch flared up, making Jack blink with the sudden light, and cough with the acrid smell of resin and turpentine.

'Help me,' said the voice.

Now in the light of the flare Jack saw the keeper of the voice.

In front of him was a big glass tank, made of thick wavy glass filled with an amber-coloured water, and inside the tank, on a throne covered in barnacles, sat a sunken king.

The King's crown was sunk deep on to his head, and his

head was sunk low on to his chest, and his chest was drooped towards his stomach and his stomach was low on his legs and his legs were deep in the water, and his feet were mired in weed.

His eyes, so set back in his head that they might have looked rearwards, regarded Jack. Such blue eyes, each like a grotto. Underwater caves of eyes that held in them deep secrets, of treasures and gold and lost ships.

The King raised his hand. The fingers were long, like stems of coral, and covered in small scales like a fish. Jack suddenly remembered how his skin had been scaly when he was reeled out of the well. He shuddered. Would he become like this sunken king?

'Come near,' said the King.

Trembling, Jack approached, determined to show no fear even though, at this moment, he was made of fear.

'You are Adam Kadmon,' said the King.

'I am Jack Snap,' said Jack.

'It hardly matters what you call yourself,' said the King. 'If you were not Adam Kadmon, you would not be here.'

'I don't want to be here,' replied Jack. 'I have been kidnapped by the Magus.'

'And it is the Magus who has imprisoned me in this tank,' said the King. 'I was his master once, and I have tried to prevent him working his evil, but I have failed. Where I have failed, you must succeed.'

'He wants to turn lead into gold,' said Jack. 'That is what the alchemists strive to do, is it not?'

'He would turn all things into gold – do you understand me, Adam, all things into gold.'

'All things into gold . . .' repeated Jack. 'He hasn't managed any of it yet – the other boys told me so.'

The King nodded. 'Once upon a time, I had power over him, and he could do nothing without my command. But he studied in secret, and chose a way that was not the Way of Light. He overcame me, and here you see me now, usurped and in prison. He cannot kill me, for there is an ancient law that prevents a servant from killing his master – even such a servant as he, dark as he. Instead he waits for me to die.'

'I could shatter the glass,' said Jack. 'You could escape with me now.'

The Sunken King shook his head, and his hair was like seaweed that flows under water. 'That will change nothing. My power must first be renewed.'

'How can that be?' said Jack.

'You must find the Dragon and bid him prepare a Bath. In those strange waters, I can be renewed. But there is not much time left for me. I am already beginning to dissolve.'

And it was true. As Jack looked at the Sunken King he saw how blurred and watery were his outlines. *The amber colour of the water is his lifeblood*, thought Jack. *He is becoming the water he sits in.*

'If the Magus is free to follow his own path,' said the King, 'ruin will follow him. There will be nothing left of life, do you hear me, Adam Kadmon? Nothing left of life.'

'My name is Jack Snap,' said Jack, and he felt it was

important to keep saying his own name, lest he too should begin to dissolve in this formless place, or grow dark in the Dark House. His name was his outline, and his own quiet light. He would be his own name.

'When you say Dragon, what is it that you mean?' said Jack.

'I mean Dragon,' said the King.

'There are no dragons,' said Jack. 'The very last dragon that ever lived was killed by St George, here in England.'

'We are in the cellars of the Dark House,' observed the Sunken King, 'yet the Dragon is lower down yet. You must dive deeper, deeper dive.'

As Jack was about to argue more about this matter of a dragon he heard a noise above him in the hall. He clapped his hands over the flare, burning himself a bit but not crying out, then moved as fast as he could back up the stairs, holding his jacket around the candle so that he could see his way but not be seen. As he got to the hall, he saw that the door to the courtyard was wide open. His heart leapt. Without thinking he dropped his candle and ran. He would be free, he would go home, he would escape. There was no more need of darkness and dissolution. No more to do with kings and creatures and boys and stone beds. He was his own Jack and he was in the courtyard under the stars, and there was the outer door to the street, and that was open too, and he had crossed the cobbles, and reached it, and he was out, and straight into the arms of . . .

The Magus.

'How now, little fish? What are you doing swimming here, eh?'

Jack struggled and he kicked and he fought, but it was useless. The Magus was strong as twenty Jacks, and soon had him bundled back through the doors into the hall and into the library where a fire was burning and the room lit.

A grey servant stood waiting for orders.

'Fetch Wedge,' ordered the Magus, and to Jack, 'So you thought you would leave me so soon? Oh no, that cannot be.'

Wedge came hopping into the room. He was dressed in half a nightshirt and wore half a bedcap on his half-head.

'Not my fault, Master, no, nothing of me, nothing of me!'

'How did this boy leave the dormitory?'

'Witchcraft, it must have been!'

'He didn't lock the door,' said Jack suddenly.

The Magus went towards Wedge. Wedge hopped backwards, and they did this all around the room, Wedge hopping backwards and the Magus going forwards, Wedge swearing on all the saints in heaven and all the devils in hell that he had locked the door as he always did.

'Took the keys off her and locked the door.'

'She gave you the wrong key, then,' said Jack, suddenly thinking that was a way to start them squabbling with each other, as well as to save himself from further search and investigation.

'Spells, it was!' cried Wedge. 'Spells, magic! Don't beat me!'

'The boy has not learnt to use his powers,' said the Magus. 'That I know to be true. If he left the dormitory, and manifestly, he did leave the dormitory, then he left not by magic, but by the door! You left it unlocked, Wedge, and for your stupidity you shall starve for three days and three nights.'

'Starve her, then!' cried Wedge. 'For She is the Keeper of the Keys, as well you know, and She gives me the key of a night to lock the door, as well you know, and I lock it according to the key . . .' He tapered off, mumbling, 'as well you know'.

'You shall both be starved,' said the Magus. 'Now get out of my sight.'

Wedge hopped towards the door and, as he passed Jack, he said under his breath in a low snarl, 'Now you have made an enemy of me, my fine lad, my Jackster. An enemy have you made!'

The Magus sat down at the round stone table and gestured for Jack to sit near him. Unwillingly Jack did so.

'I have something to show you,' said the Magus, 'that no soul here but myself has ever seen. Behold!'

The Magus opened a stone jar that sat on the stone table, and took out a handful of dust. He threw this on the fire, and the fire immediately raged up, and then changed colour, first to green, then to red, then, as the flames turned back to gold, there appeared in the flames in the fireplace, a golden city.

'London!' cried Jack.

There was St Paul's, there was London Bridge with its

56

houses and shops and golden horses going to and fro. There was Cheapside, crammed with stalls selling flowers and root vegetables, and there was Billingsgate, sizeable as a whale, selling every fish of every kind, some in tanks, some in casks, some still gasping golden on golden slabs.

There was the Strand and its printing shops, where Jack was going to be an apprentice. There were the Inns of Court. There was the Queen's palace at the Tower of London, and the bear gardens at Vauxhall. There was the river itself, the Thames, turning through the city like a bow, but in the flames it was like a golden bow, that bent past the banks and wharves of the city.

'Imagine a city made of gold, and each thing in it made of gold, and every person as golden as a precious statue, and the Thames itself a flowing golden god, where a dropped line would hook a golden fish, and where a dipped bucket would pour pure gold. Imagine it, Jack. Such a city would be the wonder of the world and the wealth of the world. A man who was king of that city would be a king indeed.'

'It is real?' asked Jack, kneeling and looking in wonder into the flames.

'It is a vision,' said the Magus. 'A vision of what shall be.'

The flames began to die back, and as they did so the golden city shrank and disappeared into the burning wood.

'So you must stay with us, Jack,' said the Magus, 'and if you are what I believe you to be, riches and power will be yours.'

'What do you believe me to be?' asked Jack.

'You are the Radiant Boy,' answered the Magus, 'the boy that is written in the ancient books of life, and when your power is added to my power, there is nothing that we shall not accomplish.'

It was almost day. Through the window Jack saw the night disappearing.

The Magus told him to go into the laboratory and stoke the furnace. 'I shall not punish you on this occasion,' he said. 'But I shall watch you closely, and I shall know what you say, what you think, what you do, and where you are. If you become a fly, I shall become a spider. If you become a mouse, you shall feel my whiskers at your tail. If you become a horse, I shall be your rider. And if you are a fish, I shall soon be your net. Run where you will, Jack, I shall not let you go.'

The Magus left the room. Downhearted, Jack went to begin his work. Then his mind went over the night's events, and the Sunken King, and what was that about the Dragon?

What dragon? He would find a way of asking Robert.

He thought of his mother at home, and how unhappy she must be. But his mother was not at home. She was in the kitchen of the Dark House with Mistress Split.

DOG DOES IT

'I won't cut it in half, whatever he says!'

Mistress Split had the little black spaniel on her knee and she was bending over it like half a mother. 'What do you call this little love, this little dove? A dog, you say? Never seen one in all my born days, not that I have born days, being made like I am and not born in the way common to all.'

Jack's mother didn't know what to say.

After she had left the house of Mother Midnight, she had felt the strong pull of the magnet and followed it as it guided her through the empty, eerie late and misty London alleys.

She could not shake off the feeling that she was being fol-lowed. Now and again she looked around, and fearfully behind her, thinking that a footpad with a pistol, or a fiend with a red face must be close behind. But she saw nothing.

At length, the heat and the vibration of the magnet inten-sifying, she wound her way through the twists and turns of deformed streets that were more like a labyrinth than a passage. She was tired, lost, losing heart, and so she sat down for a moment on a rough stone mounting-block and with the little leather magnet bag in her lap she put her head in her hands.

Something wet licked her. Something warm snuggled its

face against her face. Something made of love sent its love straight into her heart.

She opened her eyes, her hands, her heart, and there was Jack's spaniel looking up at her with his deep brown eyes.

Max!

Max jumped on to her knee, and they sat awhile, quiet and together, and the woman took the courage of the little dog, that feared nothing but only wanted to find . . .

Jack.

'We'll go together,' she said, and together they went, and came to the high forbidding walls of the Dark House, just as dawn was breaking, and just as the strangest creature on earth came hopping out of the back door with a pail of slops for the pigs.

Woof!

The Creature had dropped her pail in fright, and then, Max being just a dog and a very young dog at that, he had grabbed a bone from the pail and jumped in the air with it like a pirate with the crown jewels.

'What is before me?' said the Creature, amazed.

'A spaniel,' answered Jack's mother, now cautious and alert because the magnet was throbbing. This must be the house, this must be the place.

'Lived in this house all my born days – not that I have any born days, for I never was born, but never seen a Thing so black and beautiful and shiny and like thick bubbling tar.'

Jack's mother sensed that she must show no fear and win over this odd creature, but it was Max who bounded forward, straight through the back door, woofing with merriment, and the Creature hopping after him with her pail.

And that is how they had ended up in the kitchen.

'Lived in this house all my . . . all my what? Not my born days, no . . . what then . . . yes, my bottle days!' said the Creature, chuckling with pleasure at her own wit, 'for I was made here, in a bottle, and what I see here is all I see, and what I know here is all I know. All my bottle days, tra la!'

Jack's mother was about to say that dogs in London were as often seen as rats, but the Creature had gone back to her first thought, 'And I won't cut him in two!'

'Why would you wish to kill the poor dog?' asked Jack's mother, but the Creature was shaking her head.

'All in half, all in half, all in half.'

The door flew open and in hopped Wedge.

THE EYEBAT

J ack was pouring powder of sulphur into the top of the
alembic. Robert and Crispis were stuffing pieces of lead
into the bottom of the alembic. Poor Crispis was so small
that he could hardly lift the lead from the bucket. His curly
hair was damp with sweat.

'I wish I was a rabbit,' he said, 'then I could live in a field
and eat grass.'

Jack was up on the ladder. He came down. 'Crispis, go and
give all the boys some water. Robert and I will manage the
lead.'

'Every boy must perform his allotted task,' shouted
William.

'Not if a friend will do it for him,' said Jack. 'Go on,
Crispis.'

The tiny boy smiled with happiness. William scowled.

'Do not provoke William,' said Robert. 'I do not trust
him.'

'There's no one watching us,' said Jack.

'The Eyebat is always watching us,' said Peter, coming
across with a pile of wood for the furnace.

From across the room the Eyebat was gleaming evilly
from its jar. Crispis came trotting back with two brimming

wooden cups of water. He looked at Jack the way a sunflower looks at the sun.

'Thank you, Crispis,' said Jack, and gently turned the little boy round and sent him off. 'Don't forget the others.'

Robert splashed some of his water on his face and neck.

'Have you always been an orphan, Robert?' asked Jack.

'I must have had a mother once, for I wasn't made in a bottle like the Creature,' said Robert. 'But I came here from a ship where I was a cabin boy.'

'A ship!' said Jack. 'Did you fight any pirates?'

'Yes, and we did,' replied Robert. 'Sailing off Cadiz the Spaniards attacked us, but we fought them off, and when our guns and our ammunition and our men were exhausted, a pirate ship came and plundered us. Pirates are clever. I'd rather be a pirate than anything.'

'When we escape, let's be pirates,' said Jack.

'And get a ship and go to sea!'

'And find the treasure . . .'

'And I'll have a parrot and a pair of pistols.'

'And we won't have to turn lead into gold because we'll find all the gold in the world . . . when we escape.'

Jack was laughing, but now Robert had stopped laughing, and his face was serious and sad. 'Not anything can escape, Jack. There is no escape, that's what you don't understand. This place, the Dark House, it's not just a house like other houses are houses. It's as if . . . it's like living inside a person – the Magus is this house, Jack, we are living inside him.'

Jack was silent. He thought back to when he had woken

up in the well and wondered if he were inside a whale.

'How are we living inside him, Robert?'

Robert looked around, nervous, but the other boys were all busy at their work, except for Peter, who came closer. Robert said, 'I am the eldest here, nearly thirteen, and I have been here the longest. When I came, I was brought off the ship because my master had sold me, and I didn't think much of it, but when the cart brought me to this house, the man driving the cart, all fearful and watchful, said to me, "Boy, they have sold you to the Devil. I tell you true, this house does not exist! Look for it and it does not exist."'

'But it does exist,' protested Jack, 'we are in it, and we have both been outside it, and there is a courtyard, and last night the Magus came and went. How could he come and go if there was nothing here but a phantom?'

'It exists in his mind,' said Robert, 'and so do we.'

'I am Jack!' said Jack out loud, and William looked round. 'You are Robert! There's Peter.'

'But he is the Magus,' said Robert. 'I can think of a house, but not so that you can go inside it. He can think of a house, and we are inside it – all of us.'

'Even if that is true,' said Jack, 'and I don't believe it is true, we have a life that is not his life.'

'Do you think so?' said Robert. 'What life do we have that is not his life?'

Jack shook Robert by the shoulders. 'Stop it! Whatever this house is, we will escape. Now tell me something I want to know. Is there such a thing as, well, something like a dragon in here?'

Robert's face went white with fear. 'Who told you there was a dragon?'

'I know there aren't any dragons,' said Jack, 'but I am looking for one.'

'That's easy!' said Crispis. 'Whatever doesn't exist is nearby.'

Robert sighed and Peter cuffed the child on the head, but gently, and in play.

'As it happens,' said Robert, 'yes, we do have a dragon.'

'Where?'

'Sometimes you can see it in the dry moat that lies lower than the house, as though the house rose out of the moat and will one day fall back there. It is all wrapped around the house.'

The boys were crowding round now.

'Tell me where the dry moat is!' said Jack. 'Can we see it from here? What if we climb up to the skylight and look down?'

'It is forbidden to climb up to the skylight,' said William.

'Everything is forbidden!' said Jack. 'I don't care. Come on! Who's going to help me? I need help with the ladder!'

'We'll be punished!' said Peter.

'This is being punished!' said Jack. 'This is the worst punishment I ever had, worse than being locked in the cellar for stealing apples, worse than being beaten with a stick for breaking a window, worse than being made to row up and down the Thames all day because I stole a boat – I didn't steal it really, I just borrowed it.'

'I'm too frightened,' said Roderick.

'That's because you've all been here a long time. He's broken your spirit. You have to fight back – we can beat him.'

'You'll kill us all!' shouted William, and he rushed at Jack, but the other boys pulled him off.

'Peter! Anselm! Hold William,' said Robert. 'All right, Jack, we'll help you. Roderick, get the ladder with me!'

Reluctantly Roderick helped Robert to steady the ladder for Jack and soon Jack had shinned up and was high as the skylight.

'Robert,' he called down, 'if the house doesn't really exist, then the Dragon can't really be wrapped around it, so we're safe aren't we?'

Jack pushed open the skylight and eased his body half out on the roof. He looked out. His heart lifted; there was St Paul's cathedral spire on the skyline. He was not so far away from home.

He looked down. There was the courtyard, and beyond the courtyard, yes, there was a moat, and the moat had no water in it. There was nothing in it at all; it was a deep dug ditch.

'Get down!' shouted William, struggling to break free, his face twisted with anger and upset. 'Who do you think you are? You have no right! Get down!'

Suddenly Robert heard a noise. 'Jack! Someone's coming!'

Jack began to slide himself back through the skylight, and as he did so, he dislodged a piece of lead on the roof. There it went, bouncing and skimming down the steep pitch of the roof, off the edge, and down into the moat.

And Jack saw something very strange. As the sharp heavy bit of lead hit the moat, the moat moved – that is it rippled, the way the skin of an animal ripples, and Jack suddenly realised that he had been looking for a moat with a dragon in it, but the Dragon and the moat were the same thing . . . the Dragon was the moat and the moat was the Dragon. Whatever was wrapped around the house was alive.

But it was too late for all that now.

The metal door of the laboratory shot open like someone had fired it out of a gun. Wedge and Mistress Split were roaring on the threshold.

'Eat! Eat! Eat! Meat! Meat! Meat!'

Then Wedge saw the ladder, and Jack at the top of it. He hopped straight over, kicked the ladder away, and Jack fell straight down with a crash.

And as he fell his arm knocked the Eyebat's jar from the shelf.

There was a silence. A horrified silence. Jack lay on the floor, a bit dazed, seeing the faces above him, like in a dream.

For about a minute nothing happened. Then, like the slowest genie from the narrowest jar, green and black vapour began to swirl upwards and out into the room, with the smell of rotten eggs. William and Robert were coughing. Crispis had hidden under the table.

Up went the vapour, and as the noxious gas began to clear,

there at the bottom of the broken jar, in among the jagged pieces, lying like a moth the size of a man's hand, was the Eyebat.

Its two evil eyes swivelled round.

'Catch it!' yelled Wedge, lunging forward on his one leg, but at that split second, the Eyebat propelled itself upwards in a great whirr, and hurtled around the room so fast that no one could follow it.

Screaming with fright, Anselm and Peter hid under the table with Crispis. Robert grabbed a net and tried to grab at the thing, like a butterfly. Jack scrambled to his feet, and was at once knocked down again by a furious Wedge, purple in the face.

The Eyebat dipped, dived, then settled itself nastily in the rafters, its shining evil eyes looking down.

Wedge stared around the room, swiping randomly at the cowering boys. He pushed the broken pieces of the jar with his iron-booted toe. Then he put his half-face very close to Jack and snarled, 'Oh, you are in trouble, oh, you are in trouble, my fine lad. Eyebat out, is he? Well indeed!'

Wedge looked up to the rafters. The Eyebat looked down from the rafters. Wedge laughed his horrid half-laugh with his horrid half-mouth.

'What will the Magus say? This is thunder and strife.'

Mistress Split came forward. 'The boy will pay with his life – ha ha ha ha.'

The Eyebat flapped a little on its beam.

'Be gone, you boys!' said Wedge. 'The Magus must be brought here!'

'Live in fear!' said Mistress Split, laughing at the terror of the boys. 'Live in fear!'

As the boys filed out, Wedge grabbed Jack by the shoulder and forced him round towards Mistress Split. 'Here's the trouble. Here's all the trouble in one bag of skin and bones. Here's the one that's starving us, my dear!'

'Then punish him, my dear!' said Mistress Split.

'If we shan't eat, neither shall he!'

'Let him see what it's like to go hungry!'

Wedge let Jack go, and Jack ran, rubbing his shoulder, towards the refectory.

When he got there, the boys were eating in silence, but there was no place set for Jack. He reached for a mug of water and at that second Mistress Split's sword cleaved the mug in two, and the water spilled out over the table and floor.

'Not a drop!' she said. 'Not a drip!'

And then, she dropped her sword as fast as she dropped her evil expression. A little black dog came galloping through the door, paws underneath him, falling over. Jack nearly cried out with joy, and just managed to close his mouth, as Mistress Split intercepted the dog, and swooped him up on her arm, where he licked her half-face.

'My love my dove, my love my dove, my love my dove,' and on she went, loving and doving, until Wedge came in, furious and hot-faced.

'Halves halves, halves!' he shouted. 'All is halves!' and he tried to pull the dog from Mistress Split, who bared her teeth at him.

'Shall not split him, he's a Born not a Bottle, splitting it kills it, as well you know!'

'As well YOU know,' snarled Wedge in her face. 'Dead or alive makes no odds, halves is halves to us.'

But Mistress Split held the dog up high on her one arm in her one hand, and Wedge stumped off, reeking rage.

That's my dog! thought Jack, and then he had an even bigger shock because a new servant woman, all in grey, came in with a pitcher of soup, and she looked straight at Jack, and she was his mother . . .

SOME USEFUL
INFORMATION

The Magus was in the laboratory. He was standing examining the pieces of the Eyebat's heavy glass jar. Wedge was standing with him.

'Jackster did it, Master, not Wedge, I swear on the Queen's life, not Wedge.'

'Where is the Eyebat now?'

'Behind you,' said Wedge, humbly, though it did cross his half a brain for half a second that his master was all-powerful and should know where the Eyebat lurked.

The Magus turned. Yes, there was the Eyebat, watching from its perch. 'It is not so simple to return it as it was to free it,' said the Magus. 'While it is in the laboratory there is little enough harm that it can do, but it would be unwise to free it further, do you understand, Wedge?'

Wedge didn't understand, but he obeyed, and nodded.

'Go and prepare the boys for bed,' said the Magus.

Wedge left the room. The Magus bent down and picked up the bottom of the jar. Then he looked up towards the skylight, and frowned.

The boys were in a file at the door of the refectory. Jack's mother was clearing the table. While Mistress Split was yelling and threatening and waiting for Wedge, Jack's mother shoved something into Jack's pocket as she brushed past him.

Then the boys went up the stone stairs, Mistress Split in front carrying the blazing flare, and Wedge behind, muttering oaths and threats and curses. As Jack was last in line, he felt that these oaths and threats and curses were meant for him, which they were.

In the bedchamber, Wedge made a great fuss about examining the window, and then noisily locking, unlocking and relocking the door. 'Any person that finds himself able to pass through this door is no person but a ghost!' he shouted from the other side. 'Hear me? Dead!'

'Well said!' came the voice of Mistress Split, and the two of them, or the one of them, however it is best to describe them, went hopping back down the stairs.

Jack was sitting on his bed. He got out the hard thing his mother had pushed into his pocket; it was a leg of chicken, and round the chicken leg was a message. *I am near.*

While Jack was hungrily devouring the chicken leg, and wishing he had another, he felt someone beside him. It was Crispis with a piece of bread.

'I saved it for you, Jack,' said the little boy.

Jack smiled. 'Do you know anything about dragons, Crispis?'

'Oh, yes,' said the boy. 'The one in the moat, I've seen it.'

'Did you speak to it?'

'Oh, no,' said the boy. 'A dragon cannot be spoken to unless it speaks first. It is very ancient, and has the ancient right of speaking first.'

'Who told you this?' asked Jack.

'The Magus,' said Crispis. 'He used to love me, and when he used to love me he used to sit me on his knee and tell me things.'

'Why doesn't he love you now?' said Jack.

'I wasn't what he wanted. I wasn't the right magic.'

'What is the right magic?' asked Jack, but Crispis shook his head.

'I wish I were a heron that came to the deep pool and found the golden fish.' Then the boy fell straight asleep, just like that.

Jack laid him gently in his own bed and went and stood at the window. There were clues here if he could unriddle them. What was the truth about the boys? What was the 'right magic'? And what about the Dragon?

There was a noise at the door.

Jack bounded across on soft feet and listened. He put his eye to the keyhole and fell back, because there was another eye on the other side of the keyhole.

'JACK . . . JACK . . .'

It was his mother.

Jack speedily unlocked the door. His mother came into the bedchamber and hugged him with all her heart. Jack locked the door again and he took her by the hand and led her over to the window.

'How ever did you find me?' asked Jack.

'The magnet did lead me here. Then by some miracle, the

Creature – Mistress Split – conceived so great a longing for your dog Max, that she allowed me leave to be a servant here. I shall see you every day, and before another moon passes, I swear we shall escape, Jack.'

'Escape we shall, Mother,' said Jack, 'but we cannot forget the other boys, and there is an old king imprisoned in the cellar. And the Magus has some Work, some terrible Work I think, that will make gold out of all the world, and that is why he stole these boys, and that is why he stole me.'

'Gave he a word of explanation?' said Jack's mother.

'Yes, he tells me I am something called the Radiant Boy.'

In the clear moonlight Jack could see his mother's face cloud with alarm. 'Mother?' he said questioningly.

'Oh, Jack, remember when you were a little boy and I had a position as housekeeper in the house of John Dee? Your father lived then, and he was employed by that man to make all kinds of strange work in metal, and all under great secrecy.'

'Yes, I remember,' said Jack.

'John Dee did tell me that you were born under a fiery star at the exact conjunction in the Heavens of Jupiter and Saturn, and that although you had no magic power of your own, you were a boy where magic could happen. That is what he did tell me: "Here is a boy where magic could happen." Your father did say that was all well and good, but better to be able to unlock any lock . . .'

'And so he made me this . . .' said Jack, turning the iron tool in his hands.

'And better to find anything that needed to be found . . .' Jack's mother took out the magnet. 'These are your gifts from your own father, Jack. What gifts the unseen powers gave you, I know not.'

'Perhaps to outwit a dragon,' said Jack, and told his mother all that had passed up to that moment.

Suddenly, while they talked in whispers, there was the sound of a key in the lock of the bedchamber. Jack's mother lay flat in the dark space between Jack's bed and the window, and Jack jumped into his bed, forgetting that Crispis was there already, but the boy was so tiny that it hardly mattered.

The door opened slowly. The wavering light of a candle threw giant shadows through the chamber. Jack opened one eye; it was the Magus.

The Magus came over to where Jack was pretending to sleep, his mother prone and terrified on the floor beside him, but the Magus seemed not to notice.

'Get up, Jack, and follow me.'

Jack had to obey. Under cover of the covers he slipped his iron tool out of his pocket and left it in the bed. Then he got up, put on his jacket and shoes and followed the Magus, who locked the door after him. Jack hoped and prayed that his mother would get away.

Down the stairs went Jack, following the Magus. At the door of the Creature's room he half stopped, and half looked in, and there, as before, the Creature(s) lay half asleep.

'Why did you cleave them in two?' said Jack, suddenly.

The Magus half turned on the stair. 'I wished to know what would happen. Without experiment there is no knowledge.'

The Magus continued down the stairs, and as Jack stood in the entrance to the room, half mesmerised again, a small black bundle detached itself from Mistress Split's half-bed and half ran, half tumbled, in all its complete and black and soft self, like night sky and night stars, its eyes shining in the heavy dark of its head.

'Max!' Jack's own eyes filled with tears and fell in liquid stars on to the dog's upturned face. Max licked Jack's tears away. 'Stay here and help me, Max. Be ready and be brave and I'll try to be brave too.'

Holding the puppy to himself for half a minute, Jack put Max down and swiftly left the room. He heard a whimper that went to his heart, but he knew in his heart that Max understood him. The Magus, with his stony face, was waiting at the bottom of the stone stairs.

Jack entered the library.

Upstairs, Crispis woke up. 'Ouch!' he said.

Jack's mother got up from her position. 'Oh,' said Crispis. 'Who are you?'

'I am Anne, the mother of Jack.'

Crispis regarded her with his deep anxious eyes. 'I haven't got a mother.' Then he pulled the iron tool out of the bed, and glared at it. 'Ouch!' he said again. Jack's mother knew what it was, and gently took it from the little boy.

'Sleep,' she said, tucking him up and bending over him. 'There's nothing to be frightened of.'

'There is!' said Crispis. 'Quite a lot to be frightened of, but I'll go to sleep if you will sit with me a while. Do you know any stories?'

'I know one about a sunflower that found the sun,' said Jack's mother.

Crispis nodded. 'I wish I were that sunflower.'

'If you promise to go to sleep, I promise there will be a sunflower for you tomorrow,' said Jack's mother.

Crispis began to close his eyes. Jack's mother took his hand, and waited, warm and quiet, until the little boy's hand in hers relaxed, and he was asleep in the sunflower place of safe dreams.

Then Anne let herself out of the bedchamber and went swiftly and silently down the stairs, wondering where on earth she would find a sunflower by morning.

THE DRAGON

The Magus and Jack were in the library.

'Jack, can you turn that goblet into solid gold?'

'I cannot,' said Jack, keeping his eyes on the Magus.

'And neither can I. Yet, together, I believe we might. Put out your hand . . .'

Reluctantly Jack did so and the Magus put his own hand over Jack's. Jack felt a burning sensation like holding something hot that is getting hotter. He struggled.

'Let me go!'

But the Magus tightened his grip. Jack looked up at him and saw that he was in a kind of trance, so Jack did the only thing he could think of and let out a kick right at the shins of the Magus. The Magus let go with a yelp. Jack ran for it. In his panic as he reached the hallway, he dodged through a door and found himself face to face with the top of a tree. He didn't even think, just swung down the downward tree, breaking and falling through the colossal branches, and he found to his astonishment that he had dropped into another world.

A growing world, a green world, a huge world.

These plants weren't cabbages or sweet peas or lettuces or apples; they were quite unlike anything Jack had ever seen.

* * *

The glasshouse was hot as a hot summer day and dark as a hot summer night – not quite dark, and not the thick dark of scariness or the inky dark of a hole; in fact it was quite a light dark, as light as dark can be, like on the longest day of summer as it changes into night, and so Jack could see easily.

Drops of warm water fell on him from the leaves, and the air was so moist that it was like breathing water.

Jack looked up. Far above his head were gigantic green leaves that spread from branches thick as pillars that grew out of tree trunks too big for Jack to wrap his arms around, too big for three Jacks to wrap their arms around.

Lower down were plants with soft spongy hairy leaves, like creatures, and when Jack brushed through them he felt the hairs on the leaves touch him like whiskers.

There were palm trees that he had seen in pictures in books, their bark pale brown and rough and ribbed. He picked up a coconut from the floor, but he didn't know it was a coconut and he wondered if he had found the egg of some big creature, but what kind of creature lived here?

Jack shoved the coconut into his pocket and went on through the strange forest. And it was then that he saw an eye watching him.

A wide unblinking eye. A wide unblinking eye still like a pool is still, but deep as an underground pool is deep.

Jack opened his mouth but no words came out, which was just as well, because he was facing the very tip, the very top, of a very big dragon.

90

'Well met, Jack Snap. You have been waiting to speak to me, I know, but I know not why so.'

Jack remembered what Crispis had said about a dragon having the right to speak first, so he reckoned that it should be safe now for him to answer. 'I have indeed been waiting, for I am sure that you can answer me a question.'

The Dragon shot out a purple tongue to catch a big blue fly.

'No doubt, but what is it that you will do for me?'

Jack had no idea what should or could be done for a dragon. 'I have seen you on maps,' he said, 'in the bottom corners, where there is writing that says HERE BE DRAGONS.'

The Dragon looked pleased. 'Yes, my picture strikes fear into the hearts of men, for that is where I live – in the hearts of men. In their greed and envy and in their hoardings and hidings.'

Jack didn't understand any of this, but he had heard that dragons speak in riddles.

'What do you eat?' he asked suddenly, immediately wishing he hadn't. The Dragon looked amused.

'Are you wondering, perhaps, if I will eat you? The answer is, that I eat what there is to eat, and if Jack Snap is what there is to eat, then eat him I will. Yet, I am well provided for today. I will not speak of tomorrow.'

'Where do you come from?' said Jack, who wanted desperately to run away, but found himself unable to move. And the silly questions keep forming and foaming in his mouth like soap bubbles and he wished he would be quiet. But at the same time he had the strange thought that it was as though the Dragon was asking itself questions through him.

'I began in the world that you see before you,' said the Dragon. 'Your knowledge is very small and you did not know that once the whole world looked like this forest here, deep and dense and vast and untravelled. There were frogs as big as St Paul's Cathedral, and reptiles whose bodies were longer than the Thames. There were birds whose wingspan darkened the sun, and there were spiders whose webs were like spun cities. The tiniest fly could have carried you off as an eagle does a lamb.

'In that world, so great a heat from the sun and so great a moisture from the canopy of the trees caused a perpetual steam to rise from the floor of the forest, and from this steam creatures of every kind emerged, hunting, crying, stalking their prey. At evening the creatures of your nightmares came slowly to drink at the edge of a purple lake fringed with trees that cast odd shadows on to the water, and in whose branches hung fruit and nuts enough to feed a nation. Nuts the swell of pumpkins, sardines that would take two men to land them. Not that there were any men, for this was a time before men, and that is also a time that will come again in the far, very far distant future, when the Earth reclaims herself, as she will.

'My kind and I were plentiful. We roamed and ranged the full stretch of the Earth, and if we had continued, your kind could not have come to be.'

'The good Lord made the Earth,' said Jack, 'and everything in it within seven days.'

'Mayhap so,' said the Dragon, 'But not everything at the same time. Not everything at once. How long were seven days in those days, Jack? You cannot answer me, for you do not know.'

And Jack did not know how to answer and he was silent.

'When my kind became extinct, do you think it was so simple for us to disappear? No, not so. We disappeared from the face of the Earth only to return in the deepest lairs of men.'

'When a thing is gone it is gone,' said Jack stubbornly. 'When a house is knocked down and another built in its place, why, the first house is gone for ever.'

'Even that is not so simple as you would believe,' said the Dragon, 'for whatever has stood in the world leaves behind an imprint, an echo, a scent, a spirit. What is destroyed is also reclaimed. What has been lost waits to be found.'

Jack was out of his depth, like a swimmer who can hardly see the land. Dragons talk in riddles, yes, in riddles . . .

'Time passes,' said the Dragon, 'the clock chimes, men are born, grow old, and die, the world changes. All that is true, Jack, but that is not the sum of truth. You are young, but your deepest mind is as old as the mind of the first man who ever was, and what he saw, you can see, and what he knew, you can know, and what he feared, you fear too. You are many Jacks, many minds, many lives, but you live this one now, and that is what you see, like a man in a great house who confines himself to a single room and a single view.

'And I, I am older even than mankind, and I have seen much.'

Jack thought of the Thames, and how his mother had told

him that the Romans had rowed up the river and how in those days, so far away, the banks were thickly wooded and mammoths roamed the land. And how there were rich houses along the banks of the Thames, and the mammoths were all gone, but the river still ran its course. It was the same river. Perhaps his mind was like that river.

'Yes so, Jack Snap,' said the Dragon. 'You are like that river.'

Jack said, 'The Magus can read my mind too.'

The Dragon said, 'The Magus is able to read your mind only when you are troubled in mind. When you are asking yourself a question, or when you are afraid, or when you are in doubt, then he can read you. When you are certain, and if your mind is bold, he cannot. There, I have told you a useful secret.'

'There's an old man locked in the cellar,' said Jack, blurting things out as usual. 'He's a King, and he said I had to find you and bid you to prepare him a Bath.'

'And if I do that,' said the Dragon, 'why, what will you do for me, Jack Snap?'

Jack stood a long time. He said nothing.

'And your mother is here . . .' said the Dragon softly, 'is she not, and your dog?'

'Does the Magus know that?' said Jack, suddenly anxious in his mind.

'He does now,' said the Dragon, 'for your foolishness has told him so.'

Jack went red. 'You are the same as him!'

'Not so, Jack Snap, but something of so.'

Jack turned and tried to stumble away. He felt stupid and angry and scared. Was the Dragon really the Magus and the Magus really the Dragon? Why did the Dragon talk in riddles all the time?

The Dragon called him back. 'Jack Snap! I am the only one who can help you.'

'I can't trust you,' said Jack, 'if you are him or of him!'

'I did not ask you to trust me,' replied the Dragon, 'and if you knew anything about dragons, you would not trust me. Your trust is not interesting. You want something from me and I want something from you. That is interesting.'

'What do you want from me?' asked Jack.

'I want the Cinnabar Egg that he keeps in his bed-chamber.'

'I don't even know where he sleeps!' said Jack.

'He does not sleep,' said the Dragon, 'but you will find the Egg and bring it to me. It looks rather like that coconut you have in your pocket.'

Jack started guiltily. The Dragon knew everything. The Dragon suddenly plucked a coconut from a great palm that grew beside him, split the nut, and gave it to Jack to drink.

'Drink to our bargain,' said the Dragon, 'for that is how the race of men seals a bargain.'

Jack drank, expecting to fall down dead, but the coconut milk was delicious.

'And if I find the Egg . . . and if I bring it to you?'

'Only in the sulphur waters can the Sunken King be set free.'

SOME MORE USEFUL
INFORMATION

As Jack turned to go, the Dragon shot out a long scaly foot, and nearly frightened Jack to death.

'Why so nervous, Jack? Take these, for they will be of some use to thee. Guard them well, with dragon-care.'

And the Dragon gave Jack seven sunflower seeds. Jack dropped them into his pocket with the coconut. Then he left the way he had come, climbing the strange tree with its mossy branches that led from the Dragon's lair back up to the house.

The hallway was as dark as ever. The door to the library was open. Jack crept across the floor and saw the Magus sitting at the stone table poring over a book. He was as still as stone himself, more like a statue than a human being.

Realising that he had a chance, Jack ran back to the cellar to tell the Sunken King what had happened with the Dragon.

As he entered the cellar he was talking already. 'I have met with the Dragon! I must find the Cinnabar Egg, and then he will prepare the Bath.'

But the Sunken King gave no acknowledgement of Jack's presence. He remained in his glass tank, but he was fearfully changed. It was as though the waters had begun to claim him, and the outlines of his body wavered and vanished, vanished and wavered.

Jack went right up to the thick glass and pressed his hands against it to attract the King's attention. Curiously, for the room was cold, the glass was warm.

The King raised his head, slowly, slowly, as though he were raising himself through many lifetimes, and coming to the surface of this life, now.

'It is too late,' he said in a whisper.

'Not too late,' said Jack, 'I'll be quick as a thief, but help me, please – where does he sleep, the Magus?'

'He does not sleep,' said the Sunken King faintly, echoing the Dragon, 'yet his chamber is near your own, and there you will find the Cinnabar Egg.'

As the King said these last words his voice faded away like a ghost pulled back through time.

Jack hesitated, nodded, then ran back up the stairs. His mind was racing – if the Magus was still in the library, if Jack could discover the chamber, if he could take the Egg . . .

He was already at the foot of the first flight from the hall to the upper floors, when the library door was flung wide open and there was the figure of the Magus standing in the doorway.

'Jack . . .'

Jack turned, afraid.

'Don't be afraid, Jack, I am not going to punish you. Come back – you ran away too fast.'

Jack entered the room. There was his mother, standing

100

quite still on the far side of the table, by the fireplace.

'Did you think I would not know? Did you think I would not divine it?' said the Magus.

'Know what? Divine what?' replied Jack defiantly.

'Oh, Jack, you are cleverer than that, and I am far cleverer than you. This is your mother, Anne. She came to find you. But fear not, I shall not send her away. Indeed, I have made quite certain that she will stay with us. Come here, Jack.'

Reluctantly Jack went round to where the Magus was standing with his mother. When he saw what he saw he cried out.

His mother had been turned to stone.

'Jack, have no fear,' said his mother bravely.

Jack looked down. His mother's feet, her shins, her knees, the tops of the legs to her waist had been turned to stone. Her arms were free and her upper body was flesh.

'It is well, is it not,' said the Magus, 'that your mother should watch over you?'

Then, like a lion, the Magus seized Jack in both his hands and held him in a grip so tight that Jack thought he would burst his blood vessels. 'Jack,' said the Magus, 'you will not disobey me, you will not betray me, for the next time you do, then I will turn your mother to stone up to her neck, do you hear, and after that, if there is a third time, she will be as stone as a statue.'

'Let her go!' said Jack.

'When you become my true assistant, when you serve me as I require. When the mighty work of the Opus is complete, then on that day, I tell you, Jack, on that day and on no other, your mother will be freed to life. Do you understand, Jack? The choice is yours. Your mother's life is for you to keep or to lose!'

The Magus let go of Jack and walked towards the window, where the light was just beginning to open the black night sky.

The second the Magus turned away, Jack's mother motioned to her son, and as he came forward she slipped him the iron tool. As the Magus turned back, all he saw was the two of them embracing.

'Most touching sight,' he said, 'a mother and son.'

'Did you never have a mother yourself, sir?' said Anne, 'a mother who would do for you what I have done for Jack? 'Tis only what any mother would do.'

'My mother died in childbirth,' said the Magus. 'I never knew her. My father sold me for a gold coin.'

The Magus took a worn gold coin from his pocket and spun it into the air, where by some magic it hung for a moment like a small sun in the cold room. As it fell, the Magus caught it. 'That was my price . . .'

There was a silence in the room, such a silence as Jack had never heard. It was the silence of loss.

'And so,' said the Magus, 'I take pity on boys who like me have no father and mother, and I give them work and shelter. They shall all be rewarded in good time.'

'Jack is not a boy without mother or father,' said Anne. 'You cannot keep him.'

'He is the Radiant Boy,' said the Magus, 'and that is he for whom I have searched all these years, like my master before me. He will allow me to complete the Work.'

'I don't know how to,' said Jack.

'You will know,' said the Magus. 'Now go to the kitchen and get food and drink from Mistress Split, and bid her attend to your mother when she is done.'

Jack kissed his mother and left for the kitchen. When he pushed open the heavy oak door that led to the vast stone kitchen, he saw the fire burning in the deep hearth, and lying in front of it, black nose in velvet paws, was his dog Max.

Jack ran forward and scooped Max up in his arms, crying into his warm fur. Jack didn't cry much, he was a brave boy, but sometimes things are so awful that tears are all you can do. If he hadn't cried then, not for himself but for his mother, what kind of a boy would he have been? A boy without a heart.

But Jack had a heart; a big brave beating heart, and it was his heart that wept. His dog Max licked his tears away and tried to show Jack that he wasn't alone and sad.

Sunflower seeds, Cinnabar Egg, Sunken King, Dragon, Magus, gold, gold, gold . . . all the names and images were whirling around in his head that felt too hot from the fire and from his misery. He sat down on the stone floor, a picture of dejection, feeling suddenly helpless and hopeless. What could he do? He was only a boy.

The kitchen door crashed open and in hopped Mistress

Split. She was in a state of high glee, and singing to herself:

'All mine, all mine, all the time, all the time.'

She pulled her sword from her skirt and swung it over her head to the hanging metal rack where the pots and pans hung. She used the sword like a stick, and beat the pots and pans like cymbals, hopping up and down, crash bang slam, crash bang slam. 'All mine, all mine, all the time, all the time!'

Suddenly she noticed Jack sitting on the floor with his knees drawn up, and Max sitting beside him. Her half-face was a picture of contradictions. When she looked at the dog, her face was soft as milk. When she looked at Jack, her mouth was stretched like a fox that finds its prey.

'Now SHE is done for, the dog is MINE! Never had a whole mine all my Bottle days. Never had more than a half of this or a half of that or a half of the other. Now I have a dog entire – four paws, two eyes, two kidneys, all a nose, and all MINE.'

She hopped over to the fireplace in a giant leap and cuffed Jack out of the way, scooping up the unfortunate Max, who knew enough to pretend enough to save the boy he loved.

'Boojie Boojie Boojie!' said Mistress Split.

Jack got up and placed himself out of reach.

'Who told you to come meddling in my kitchen?' demanded Mistress Split, her half-nose in Max's full furry neck.

'The Magus,' said Jack evenly, refusing to show fear. 'His orders were to feed me and then to attend to Mistress Anne.'

'Your mother, eh?' said Mistress Split. 'No more mother now! And no more dog!'

'That is my mother's dog, not my dog,' said Jack.

Mistress Split came forward and thrust her half-face in his face. 'MY DOG,' she said.

Jack did not flinch. 'Please do as the Magus says. Those are his orders – to feed me, to attend to my mother, and . . .' Jack had had a brainwave. Suddenly he knew how he could locate the secret bedchamber of the Magus. '. . . and you are to service his chamber.'

Mistress Split snorted. 'Does he think I have more than half a pair of hands? Get your own bread and cheese, go on, and put the same on a tray for your mother, if I am to take it to her. As to the chamber . . .'

Wedge came slamming into the kitchen, the look on his face like half a thunderstorm. 'KEYS!' he yelled.

'If you PLEASE,' yelled back Mistress Split.

'Boys must rise and be earnest,' said Wedge.

'The Magus wants his chamber serviced,' said Mistress Split.

Wedge scowled. 'What time have I to do that today?'

Mistress Split shrugged. 'Orders is orders, that's his way.'

She flung the keys across the table and balanced the tray deftly on one hand. She left the room, Max trotting beside her.

'I'll have that dog in two!' said Wedge. 'All halves, as well She knows, all halves, no wholes, as well She knows.'

Then he stopped talking to himself and fixed Jack with a

dark stare. 'You! Come with me. The boys must be woken and I'll not leave you to yourself, mischief Jackster.'

Jack followed Wedge upstairs to the boys' chamber.

What was puzzling Jack was where the door to the Magus's chamber could be, for there were no doors but one on the top landing where the boys slept, and yet the Sunken King had said that this was the place.

Wedge unlocked the door and lined the boys up in order of age. Crispis, rubbing his eyes and still sleepy, came last.

As Wedge was hurling oaths and threats of punishment at the boys, who were hastily making their beds or pulling on their socks, Jack told Crispis to watch where Wedge went as the boys filed downstairs. Usually this only took place with Wedge at the rear and Mistress Split at the head, but today was different . . .

Sure enough, Wedge ordered the boys to go straight to the laboratory and begin making the fires. There was always two hours' hard work chopping wood and heating water before breakfast.

The boys set off meekly. Crispis trailed at the rear, and at the last second looked round to see Wedge doing something very strange indeed . . .

HOW TO KEEP A PROMISE

In the laboratory Jack told Robert and Peter what had happened the night before; how he had met the Dragon, and been instructed to steal the Cinnabar Egg. William was listening. 'You'll never find it if it's in his chamber. Nobody knows where his chamber is.'

'Yesterday Robert thought I could never find the Dragon, but I did so,' said Jack. William frowned. The Eyebat flew past with a whoosh.

'I hate that thing,' said Robert.

'If the Magus ever finds out that you are planning to escape . . .' said William.

'Who is going to tell him?' said Jack defiantly. 'I am going to find the Egg, free the Sunken King, and then the Magus will be defeated.'

'But he has turned your mother to stone!' said Robert.

'The King will return her, I know he will,' said Jack. 'He will do that if I save him and restore his power.'

Crispis came forward. 'Your mother promised me a sunflower this morning,' he said sadly.

'How did she do that?' said William suspiciously, and just as Jack was about to say that he had unlocked the door to his mother, he saw the look on William's face, and he knew he must not trust him.

Robert simply shrugged his shoulders; he was used to Crispis saying strange things. 'We had better get to work,' he said, 'before Wedge comes back. William – fire the furnace, Jack, bring mercury for the alembic, Crispis, tell the others to chop the wood.'

William turned away to his tasks. Crispis came up to Jack. 'It's in the ceiling,' he whispered. 'I saw it.'

And he told Jack what had happened . . .

Wedge had stood in front of the door to the boys' chamber, and using his stick, he had rapped three times on the ceiling above the door. As Crispis had lingered, hiding behind the newel post on the stairs, he had heard a click and seen a small trapdoor open in the ceiling. More than that he had not seen, because Wedge, suspicious, had suddenly looked round, but he could not see tiny Crispis, thin as an adder, slithering flat on his bottom down the stairs.

'Excellent!' said Jack. 'And I have something for you. Look.' He took a sunflower seed from his pocket. 'Here is your sunflower, Crispis. A promise is a promise.'

'That is not a sunflower!' said Crispis.

'Yes it is. Inside this seed is a sunflower.'

'How can I get it out?' asked Crispis.

'Soil and water,' said Jack. 'Plant it and you will have a sunflower. But for now, hide it in your pocket. Quick – it's Wedge.'

It was Wedge and Mistress Split fetching the boys for breakfast. But there had been a change; now the two of them snarled and scowled at each other as much as they ever did at the boys.

In the refectory Jack slid on to the bench beside Robert.

'Tonight I'm going to break into the Magus's chamber. Will you help me?'

'I don't know,' said Robert. 'It's hopeless.'

'If you say it's hopeless then it will be hopeless!'

'He knows everything we do.'

'The Dragon told me that he only knows what we are thinking when we are anxious or afraid. If we aren't afraid we'll succeed.'

'I am afraid,' said Robert.

'All I want you to do is to keep watch while I am in his chamber. If anyone comes upstairs or anything happens, can you hoot like an owl?'

Robert nodded.

'Tonight, then, Robert, promise me?'

'But we'll be locked in!'

William came and sat by them, listening. Jack fell silent.

The day passed as the days did in the Dark House. The boys worked at the alembics, Crispis sat sleepily nodding by the talking Head that never talked. The Eyebat whooshed about, but no one took any notice of it any more.

The Magus was strangely absent, and Jack felt sure that

something was being prepared. The heavy lead-like quality of the days that passed without any change had a different feel today, like light on a cold floor. Jack knew that the Magus would know that he had spoken to both the Dragon and the Sunken King, but he was sure that the Dragon would guard the secret of the Cinnabar Egg because he wanted it for himself. He thought about what the Dragon had said about their bargain: 'Your trust is not interesting. You want something from me and I want something from you. That is interesting.'

It would be the same with the Magus. At present Jack was safe because he had something – even though he had no idea what it was – that the Magus wanted. Therefore there was nothing to fear. Therefore, this was the time to act.

Jack's mind settled as he turned these things over and over. He was not sure about Robert, because Robert had too much fear, but he felt sure about Crispis, a child so odd that he was true. William . . . no, Jack couldn't trust William, and he had nothing that William wanted. Therefore, William was dangerous.

At that moment Jack looked up and there was William, looking at him, with the Eyebat hovering just above his head. Quickly William averted his gaze, but Jack had seen the way he looked – envy and anger.

Jack made an effort to blank his mind now, as anxiety was creeping in, and that, he knew, made him vulnerable to the Magus.

* * *

In his library, the Magus was reading. The table was piled with books. Anne, standing quite still, could see that the Magus was consulting astrological tables.

'At the next full moon the moon will eclipse the sun,' said the Magus.

'What does that mean, sir?' said Anne.

The Magus did not answer. He turned and passed his hand over the fire, and what Anne could not see was the spire of St Paul's burning fierce gold in the flames.

The day began to close, as days must, so that even the worst days will end and bring in their ending the chance of a new start.

The boys had been sent upstairs early, and after they had talked awhile, they one by one fell asleep. Only Jack lay awake. Wide awake.

When he was sure that the house was silent, and when he had counted the boys' snores, he carefully swung himself out of bed and went to the door. He looked through the keyhole – the landing was empty. Without a sound, Jack took out the iron tool and jiggered the lock. The door was open.

Jack went to where Robert was sleeping and woke him roughly, shaking his shoulder.

'No,' said Robert, sleepily.

'Yes,' said Jack. 'Get up! You promised.'

Robert did as he was told, and to his amazement, Jack opened the door to their bedchamber.

'It isn't locked!' said Robert, now fully awake.

But Jack wasn't going to tell anyone how that had happened.

On the dark landing the two boys looked around.

'Let me stand on your shoulders,' said Jack.

While Robert was protesting, Jack balanced on the banister rail, then climbed on to Robert's shoulders. Jack was nimble and light and Robert was bigger and sturdier, so it was easy enough for the two boys. Balancing himself carefully, Jack began to feel his way across the ceiling, ordering poor Robert to walk left and right, while Robert, with his head down, held Jack's ankles, and tried to stop himself trembling with fear.

At length, Jack found what he was looking for – his hands touched on a square shape recessed into the ceiling plaster. This was the opening, but there must be some kind of a spring somewhere. Jack pushed and tested, and heard something clicking. Excited, he pushed with all his force, and suddenly the ceiling panel opened, and Jack came tumbling down off Robert and the pair of them collapsed in a noisy heap on the floor.

Jack looked up – there was the way into the Magus's Chamber.

'We'll be caught now,' said Robert. 'We'll wake the Creature.'

Robert scrambled up and ran back into the boys' bedchamber and flung himself into bed. No one seemed to be awake but Crispis.

'Robert! Come back! You have to help me!' said Jack, but

114

Robert absolutely would not get out of bed.

'Did you find the way in?' asked Crispis, appearing on the landing.

'Yes, but I can't reach it without Robert,' said Jack, in despair.

'Reach what?' said William, and Jack was not pleased to see that William too was awake. But it was too late now, and William was also on the landing, staring up at the opening.

'I will help you,' he said. 'You can climb on my shoulders. I am nearly as tall as Robert.'

Now Jack did not want to do this, but he knew he had to do something, so, holding his doubts at bay so as not to disturb his mind and let in the Magus, Jack climbed up on William's shoulders, reached into the opening, and hauled himself up with all his strength.

It was dark.

But what was the 'it' that was dark?

Jack had exactly the same feeling as he had had in the well, when he'd wondered if he had been swallowed by a whale, and at the same instant he remembered what Robert had said about how the house didn't really exist, but that they were all living inside the Magus.

'No,' said Jack involuntarily to himself.

He took a tinderbox from his pocket and struck a light. The room lit up, and in the flare Jack saw a desk with a candlestick on it. He lit the candle and looked about him.

The room was not a room at all . . .

THE PHOENIX

I t was a nest.

Jack nearly fainted with the stench – a strong, thick stench of talons and wings and hunting breath, like an owl, like a kestrel, like a hawk, like a bird of prey.

Jack tried not to breathe, but even with his handkerchief over his mouth the smell was overwhelming. Bird droppings were piled in the corners, mixed with bones and straw and dried leaves.

Feathers and dust, dusty feathers, cobwebby feathers littered the rough floor and layered it, a foot deep. The feathers were crimson and gold. Jack picked one up, wondering at it. There was no window in the room, for the room was really the closed attic of the house, and seemed to run on for miles into the dark, but there was a rough opening in the gable-end wall. Jack went over and leaned out – yes, he was right in the roof, near enough to the stars, and high above the courtyard with the well. He was glad of the sudden rush of fresh air, and sat back in the hacked-out opening, careless of the drop. He gazed into the room.

The desk was the only piece of furniture, the only sign that anything human ever came here. And the desk, unlike every-where else, was carefully dusted, polished even, with a quill pen made from one of the red and gold feathers, and a jar of red ink. There was an open book on the desk. Jack took a deep breath of clean air and made his way carefully across the room.

The page of the book had a drawing on it, and the drawing was of a phoenix, red and gold, and rising out of a smouldering heap of ashes. Standing by the phoenix was a shining boy. Jack looked at the drawing. The writing was in Latin, but on the open page, someone had written, in English, under the Latin tag:

The Radiant Boy shall free the Phoenix and the Phoenix shall find the City of Gold.

Jack looked closer. At the foot of the page was a drawing of a dragon, and at the top of the page were the spires and domes of the City of Gold.

Jack turned back the pages of the book, and there, to his horror, were drawings of all of the boys he knew – Robert, William, Anselm, Crispis, Peter, Roderick – and of other boys he had never known, and each of them had been carefully ruled through, like a mistake.

Hardly daring, but knowing without knowing what he would find, Jack turned the pages forward, and there was a drawing of himself, and at his head was a kind of halo such as he had seen in pictures of saints. But Jack knew he was no saint. He read the tag under the drawing: *The Radiant Boy.*

And as Jack looked at the picture of himself, a very odd thing started to happen. Right next to him in the picture, now strong, now faint, appeared a young girl, about his own age. Underneath her was written: *The Golden Maiden.* He turned the page – there she was, on her own page, holding a jewelled clock in both hands, and looking straight at him. Jack had the strangest feeling that he knew her – that he had always known her, but that was impossible. As he gazed, he said to himself, out loud, not knowing why, but by a strange impulse, 'Golden Maiden of the Book, if you are in the world as I am in the world, find me, help me. I am calling you. I am the Radiant Boy.'

And he had a clear image of himself standing in front of a door and that the door opened.

This is a mystery, thought Jack. *But I must keep my mind on my task.*

The Egg, he must find the Egg. A bird would have an egg, but where would it be?

Somewhere soft and safe, thought Jack, and began sifting through the feathers on the floor.

Nothing, nothing, nothing.

If I were a bird, thought Jack, *where would I hide my precious egg?*

Then Jack looked up. High, that was where a bird would hide an egg, high.

Sure enough, in the rafters, there was a kind of woven basket, long and shallow, like a fisherman's flat basket for herrings. Jack climbed on the desk, and using all his strength, he pulled himself up on the roof rafter, and dangling there, half his body hauled up, and the other half swinging, reached into the nest. At that very moment, he heard an unmistakable flapping noise coming towards the room.

The Phoenix!

Jack let go of the rafter as if it had stung him, dropped on all fours on to the desk, blew out the candle, and dived under the desk in the dark.

For a moment or two nothing happened, except for the flapping noise swooping and retreating beyond the wall. Then with a great rush of air the bird landed in its nest.

All Jack could see were strong scaly golden legs and cruel capable feet.

The bird stopped quite still in the middle of the room, then with a short hop it jumped up on to the chair behind the desk. Now, terrified as he was, Jack could see its crimson plumage and its steep strong throat.

The bird seemed to be turning the pages of the book, then, with its beak, it took the quill pen and began to write. Jack could hear the scratch, scratch, scratching of the nib.

He wanted to sneeze. More than life itself he wanted to sneeze. The feathers were in his nose. He must think of a world where everyone was born without noses and therefore could not sneeze. He held his poor nose tight between his finger and thumb, and felt his whole body cover itself in sweat at the effort of not sneezing.

Just as he thought he would either die by sneezing because the bird would find and kill him, or die of suffocation by not sneezing, the scratching sound of the quill ceased, and the bird, without a pause, spread its wings and glided effortlessly across the room and out of the window.

Jack let out such a sneeze that every single feather on the floor lifted and settled again. He sneezed so hard, that Crispis, dozing patiently on the landing below, was knocked off his feet, and had to get up again, which he did, to find that William had gone . . .

THE CINNABAR EGG

J ack had relit the candle and was reading the book.
The ink was still wet. The Phoenix had drawn a picture
and the picture was of Jack's mother turned to stone.

Jack shuddered, but he did not falter. He stood up on the
desk as boldly as he could, swung up, and reached into the
high basket.

Yes!

He felt the oval in his hand, and carefully lifted it out,
letting himself drop back to the desk, and then on to the
floor.

In the light of the candle, Jack examined his prize.

But it wasn't an egg; it was a solid gold box in the shape of
an egg.

Jack turned it over and over. This was a casket, but where
was the lock?

Jack got out his iron tool and spread out the keys and
levers. Hadn't his father said that this tool could open locks?

But what if he couldn't find the locks?

And then Jack remembered something . . .

He was seven years old, and living with his mother and
father in the house of the alchemist John Dee.

Jack had been looking at some pictures of King Arthur and the Knights of the Round Table, and one of the pictures showed Arthur as a young boy pulling the sword Excalibur from the stone. All the other men and boys, bigger and stronger, older, richer, cleverer, of high birth, had failed and failed, no matter how hard they tried. Then Arthur came, and the sword pulled clean into his hands.

John Dee, who liked Jack, and let him look at his books, had come into the room. He had taken the book from Jack and pointed to the picture – a ring on each finger, just like the Magus.

'Do you see how the others failed?' John Dee had said. 'They failed because they were concentrating on the stone and not on the sword. They saw the difficulty, but Arthur saw the sword.'

Jack stood still with the golden egg-box in his hands. Inside was the Egg, he knew it. He must not let himself be hypnotised by the difficulty, he must see through the difficulty to what it was he needed to find. He ran his fingers over the smooth surface of gold, and suddenly, under his rough little finger, was the tiniest indentation. Jack caught his breath, and rifled among the keys and levers of his iron tool. Was this one the right size? A lever like a needle? No, it was too big. He tried again, and this time chose the smallest key, a key so fine it was like a pin. But it was too big.

In the candlelight, not knowing why, Jack said, 'Father . . .' and as he spoke his father's name, he spread the levers and keys again, and saw what he had never seen before – a key fine as a hair, made from pure gold.

Jack slid the golden key into the golden lock and the golden lid of the golden box clicked open.

And there it was – big and heavy and beautiful and shining and red and orange and purple and brown all gleaming together. It was the Cinnabar Egg.

Like a flash Jack stowed the Egg into his shirt and left the room as fast as he could. He was in such a hurry that he just jumped straight down on to the landing.

He looked around. The landing was empty. Where was Crispis? Where was William?

Filled with foreboding, Jack tiptoed slowly into the boys' chamber. All was dark and quiet.

As he stepped fully inside and was about to go over to Robert's bed, he heard a familiar hateful voice.

'Jackster been exploring? Good morning!'

It was Wedge. And beside Wedge was William, grinning like a merry-go-round monkey.

'Why did you tell him, William?' said Jack.

'I was the one, not you,' said William. 'Before you came, I was the one.'

'I don't want to be the one,' said Jack. 'I want to leave here and never come back.'

'Not leaving us yet, Jackster, that I know,' said Wedge. 'Now give it to me.'

'Give what to you?' said Jack, looking directly at Wedge.

'The Cinnabar Egg. I want the Egg.'

'I shall give it to the Magus, not to you,' said Jack.

'Oh, you don't want to do that, my Jackster. You want to give it to me, and we'll say no more about it.'

'He is your master.'

'That could change,' said Wedge. 'William and myself could be the master, joint master, we could if we had that Egg.'

'Then why didn't you get the Egg for yourself, long ago?' said Jack.

Wedge looked shifty. 'I found the nest and found the box, don't think I never did, but I couldn't open the box, no one could, not ever, none of them and you weren't the first to try, some of the boys tried too, the ones that are turned to stone, you've seen them, that was their punishment, but that is in the past now, Jackster, like our little disagreements and fallings out, yours and mine. I knew you were a special boy when I saw you, and so I will make a bargain with you, handsome and fair: Give me the Egg and I will let you out and away through the courtyard door and you'll never be seen again.'

Jack hesitated.

'What about my mother?'

'I'll bring her to you in a cart. She can't walk far, it's true, on account of her legs being turned to stone, but she can sit at home with you and do sewing, yes, women like to sew. You can be free, Jackster.'

'Can I come with you?' said a piping voice.

It was Crispis.

Jack looked at the little boy and smiled. 'Yes, always, I

128

promise.' He turned to Wedge. 'Here is the Egg,' he said. And from his pocket he pulled out the coconut he had found in the Dragon's den.

Now Wedge had never seen the Cinnabar Egg, and he had never seen a coconut either. But the coconut looked egg-shaped enough, and exotic enough, and its brown hairy shell seemed to him to be the safe protection of whatever was inside.

Wedge stretched out his hand. Jack drew back.

'How do I know that I can trust you?' said Jack.

'Trust me, Jackster? Swear on my heart, I do, that trust me you can.'

'You've only got half a heart,' said Crispis, 'so Jack can only half trust you.'

Wedge glared at the tiny child. 'Halves is as good as wholes,' he said.

'And if I give you this Egg,' said Jack, 'what will you do with it?'

Wedge's eye filled with greed, 'Hatch it, Jackster, hatch it.'

'What's in it?' asked Jack. 'It's only a bird.'

'If there is nothing in it,' said Wedge, 'you wouldn't have gone to so much trouble to get it!'

'I didn't get it for myself,' said Jack, 'I got it for the Dragon.'

'The Dragon? You don't ever want to trust a dragon, Jackster, believe me, yes, believe me you should.'

'I don't trust the Dragon,' said Jack.

Wedge nodded. 'If you give me that Egg, you'll be on

your way home with your mother by midnight tonight.'

'Then I'll give you the Egg at midnight tonight,' said Jack.

'Now!' said Wedge, lunging forward. 'I say now!' But Jack was too quick for him, and ran to the window.

'I shall drop it and smash it,' said Jack.

Wedge held up his hand. 'Do it your own way we will, Jackster. I'll come for you at midnight tonight.'

Wedge hopped away, leaving Jack, Crispis and William in the bedchamber.

'Now you'll go away,' said William, 'and the Magus will choose me.'

'No he won't,' said Crispis, 'you'll see.'

'Everyone knows you are stupid in the head,' said William. 'I don't care what you say.'

'Leave him be,' said Jack. 'He is no harm to you. Crispis! We might as well go and start the fires.'

'You can't,' said William. 'We aren't allowed to leave the chamber until Wedge comes for us!'

'I don't think that Wedge is going to say much about it this morning, do you?'

And Jack took Crispis by the hand and went downstairs.

As they passed the Creature's room Jack glanced inside, and there was Mistress Split fast asleep, snoring her half snores, the dog Max lying beside her. Max saw Jack and lifted his ears, but Jack put his finger to his lips, and the dog understood.

* * *

The dark sky was breaking into pieces of morning. There was not much time.

'Crispis, we're going to take the Cinnabar Egg to the Dragon.'

'No,' said Crispis. 'I shall be eaten.'

'No you won't, we've got something he wants.'

The hallway was silent. Jack pushed open the door that led to the downward tree and, putting Crispis on his back, climbed down as he had before. The child looked in wonder at the wide, thick fleshy leaves, and deep-coloured blossoms. Once they had reached the Dragon's lair, Crispis bent down and felt the warm moist soil, and while Jack was pushing ahead, Crispis filled both his pockets with soil. He had had a good idea.

Jack didn't notice that Crispis had fallen behind. He was looking for the Dragon.

From beneath the vast trunk of a vast tree, a single eye opened, and the Dragon coughed.

'How so, Jack Snap, come back?'

Jack whirled round. The Dragon could camouflage himself easily in the prehistoric forest, and it was only his bright eye that alerted Jack to his presence. His purple and green scaly coat was hidden beneath the purple and green of the forest.

'Here is the Cinnabar Egg,' said Jack, pulling it from his shirt.

The Dragon opened both his eyes. He sat up. He sat up twenty feet high above the ground, and his long neck arched and stretched, then swooped down right at the level of Jack's head. Jack did not flinch, even though the Dragon's breath smelled of wet cloth and rabbits.

'How so, how so! Clever boy, cleverer than I guessed,' said the Dragon. 'Ah, Jack, we have a bargain indeed!'

'Why do you want this Egg?' asked Jack boldly, though once again he had the strange sensation that he only asked the questions the Dragon, in his vanity, wanted to answer.

'An Egg has two uses and that is all,' said the Dragon, 'Eat or hatch.'

'Which is it?' said Jack, marvelling that he dared to speak at all, let alone in this familiar way, to a Dragon.

The Dragon's eyes flickered and hooded themselves. He was ancient and cunning. 'Ah, Jack, hatch. A waste of such an Egg to consume such an Egg.'

'What is inside the Egg?' said Jack.

'I did not ask that question!' The Dragon pulled himself up, and shot his purple tongue into the air. 'Until now you have asked only the questions that I wanted you to ask – that is a Dragon's way. How so, Jack, that you ask a question I did not ask?'

So Jack was right. The Dragon could put words into his mouth.

'I don't know,' said Jack, truthfully, and the Dragon looked thoughtful.

'You are more than you seem, Jack Snap, and we shall meet again, both changed.'

Jack didn't know what the Dragon meant by this, so he

decided to proceed with what he did know.

'Will you prepare the Bath now, for the Sunken King?'

'I will,' said the Dragon. 'In three days' time come here again and the Bath will be prepared, and the King will be waiting for you. And I shall be waiting for you, Jack Snap. Now, the Egg.'

'How do I know that –'

'You can trust me?' interrupted the Dragon. 'You are a human being and you talk of trust. I am a Dragon who knows more of the human heart than you. Our bargain is our bargain, and by my ancient oaths I must honour it. I will tell you something, Jack Snap: trust only those you love, and for the rest, make bargains. You cannot trust the world, but you can bargain with it. Hear me, Jack: trust only those you love.'

'What do you know of love?' said Jack, who felt the Dragon asking this question.

'A great deal,' said the Dragon, 'but it was a long time ago, when love and trust grew in the world as easily as trees and flowers. Now it is otherwise, Jack Snap. Now go.'

And Jack held out the Cinnabar Egg, and the Dragon inclined his ancient head and took the Egg in his jaws.

Jack bowed – he did not know why – and walked backwards until he felt safe enough to turn, conscious of the jewel-eyes of the Dragon upon him.

As he reached the foot of the downward tree, he heard a rustle, and there was Crispis, creeping out from under a giant leaf, trembling and covered in earth. Jack grabbed him and together they climbed away.

RUMOUR

In the laboratory that day there were whispers that the Magus had a new captive. Wedge and Mistress Split had been overheard talking.

But who was it?

'It must mean that you have failed, Jack, like the rest of us,' said Robert. 'He only brings a new one when the others have failed. He tried us all in turn and we could not complete the Work.'

'I hope I have failed,' said Jack.

'Only when the Work is done can we leave,' said Robert dismally.

'William thinks the Magus will choose him,' said Jack.

Robert shook his head. 'That is because he is his son.'

Jack looked at Robert in astonishment. 'You said that all of you were orphans.'

'William is an orphan now. His mother is dead and the Magus disowned him when he could not complete the Work. He made him come here with the rest of us. He used to live in the house and be waited on by Wedge and Mistress Split. William loves his father but he hates him too.'

'A boy in half,' said Jack thoughtfully.

'What do you mean?' said Robert.

'He is divided against himself, don't you see, Robert? That's what the Magus does. He did it to the Creature and he did it to his own son. William doesn't know whether he loves or he hates, so he has no power. Half of him goes down one alley, and half down the other. The Magus doesn't want anyone to have power except for himself. None of you have power because you are all split in half too.'

'I don't know what you are saying,' said Robert.

'You don't want to be here, but you are all too frightened to leave. So you do nothing. That is what he wants. Now I think I know him a little.'

Robert was looking worried. 'You can't defeat him, Jack.'

But Jack didn't answer.

In his bedchamber, Wedge was half-whistling a half-song.

'Let HER keep the dog, and I shall keep the Egg.

She shall ask for mercy and I shall make her beg.

Once was all halves, now 'tis all wholes,

Wedge shall have the power, and SHE shall have . . .'

And he laughed, 'Nothing at all!'

Wedge went and looked at the picture of the green lion that dripped gold. 'And we won't need you either, there will be no animals when Wedge rules. Whoever heard of a green lion? You shall join the Magus in the cellar!'

And Wedge thought back to the time when the Magus had created them, him and her, but they weren't a him and her, they were just the Creature, and they were happy, and they had done his bidding; and then, one day, for something and

138

nothing – he couldn't half remember, he only half remembered – then the Magus had taken them, and split them in two, and now, and now, and now?

'She thinks more of the dog than She do of me,' said Wedge bitterly, 'and She my other half. I'll show her. Yes I will. She'll be sorry soon enough, when I am master here!'

And Wedge sat down on the edge of the bed, and shed one single tear from his one single eye, because, truth to tell, he was lonely.

'Boojie Boojie Boojie!' sang Mistress Split in the kitchen, feeding Max chicken from a plate. 'Never been so happy, not never, not ever, never had a Whole Dog to Myself! Mine mine mine, all the time time time.'

Then she got up. 'Time to feed the Captive.'

THE CAPTIVE

The Captive was sitting disconsolately looking out of the window into the empty courtyard below.

She had no idea where she was, though she knew she was in England, probably in London, and definitely in the past. At least, to her it was the past, because she lived in the twenty-first century. To everyone living here now, it was the present.

How had she come to be in this place? She went over it again in her mind. What exactly had happened?

She had been in her little bedroom, in her big rambling house; an old house, a house that contained many secrets. A house that had been in her family for hundreds of years. In a way, she lived in the past every day, because the house was so old.

She had been reading a book and fallen fast asleep, but then she had woken quite suddenly out of a dream where a boy she had never met, who said his name was Jack, was knocking at the front door and asking her to come and help him.

The second she woke up, she heard knocking at the front door. Without thought and without fear, she had gently shoved aside her big ginger cat that always slept on her bed, and got up and crept downstairs. The house was deathly quiet; everyone else was asleep. She had gone to the huge oak front door and opened it. A great gust of wind blew in, but there was no one outside, and the large untidy garden was night-time quiet.

A dream . . . always a dream.

As she had turned to go back upstairs, she had noticed a light coming from the library. She wasn't scared at all – this was her house, and she loved it. Its name was Tanglewreck, and her ancestor Roger Rover had built it in 1588 on land given to him by Queen Elizabeth the First. This was where she felt she belonged, had always belonged, and there was nothing to fear.

She had gone straight into the library.

She was astonished by what she saw.

The fire in the big stone fireplace was burning bright and high, lighting the whole room. Over the fireplace the portrait of her ancestor, Sir Roger Rover, in the ruff and jewelled doublet, seemed to be watching her closely. As she walked towards the fireplace, she saw that inside the fire, or made of the fire itself, was a golden city – domes, bridges, spires.

'What's this?' she said to herself, but out loud. 'Is this another adventure?' For truth to tell it was not the first time that the girl had found herself at the start of a strange situation . . . she was that kind of girl, and the house was that kind of house.

As she watched in wonder, a drawbridge, flaming and

shining, lowered itself from the fire, into the room, and stood at her feet. The bridge seemed solid, but also molten, like something from a volcano. None of this fire burned; rather, she felt cool, like night, like rain.

As she looked into the fire, she saw the figure of the boy in her dream. He was beckoning her, and she felt hypnotised by his clear burning eyes.

She stepped forward, on to the flaming drawbridge, into the city, through the fire, and walked unscathed into another room, another fireplace, where a woman, half-stone, half-flesh, seemed to be sleeping where she stood, and where a man so dark that he seemed to be his own night, sat at a stone table reading.

'I am the Magus,' he said, standing to his feet as she appeared, 'but who are you, and who called you here?'

She could not tell him because she did not know, and some instinct warned her to say nothing of the dream of the boy called Jack.

After the Magus had questioned her, and after she had explained that she lived in the twenty-first century, and had walked through the fire to come here, without knowing why, the Magus had brought her to this high upper room, and locked the door. She had tried to escape by every means possible – she had even climbed halfway up the chimney and met an angry jackdaw sheltering from the rain. But the chimney narrowed, she could see that, and she could not climb further.

And now she sat, covered in twigs and wood soot, staring

into the rainy courtyard.

Where on earth am I? she thought to herself.

The door flew open and in hopped Mistress Split with a beautiful black spaniel at her heel.

'And who on earth is this?' said Silver out loud.

'Woof!' barked the dog, running to greet her.

'Boojie Boojie Boojie!' sang Mistress Split, crashing the tray of food down on the table in front of Silver.

HEART OF STONE

The day passed. Night came. In the deep of the night, Jack heard the voice of the watchman far away. 'Twelve o'clock and all's well.'

Jack was ready. With Crispis beside him, he went down the stairs to meet Wedge.

He did not believe that Wedge would let him escape, but he hoped that by giving Wedge the coconut, he could distract him enough to keep his half-mind and sharp eye on other things, while the Dragon prepared the Bath for the Sunken King. Jack had decided that if by any miracle Wedge did let the three of them escape, then once his mother and Crispis were safely home, he would return and hide himself in the house until he could somehow defeat the Magus, with the help of the Sunken King. Then the other boys could be free.

'I wish I could vanish,' said Crispis, 'and be a cloud instead of a boy.'

'You'll be safe again,' said Jack, 'I promise.'

There was a noise. A door opened. Jack saw Wedge's angular silhouette in the lit doorway of the dining room.

Wedge came hopping across the hall.

'The Magus is occupied this night. He dines out with another like him, and will not return this night.'

'Where is my mother?' asked Jack.

'In the cart. She is waiting for you in the courtyard, Jackster. Follow me, and be silent!'

Jack and Crispis followed Wedge to the courtyard. Sure enough, in the cool night air, under the stars, was a cart covered with sacking. A driver dressed in black sat at the reins of a dark pony.

'How do I know my mother is in the cart?'

Wedge sneered or snarled, and flung back the sacking at the foot of the cart. Sure enough, there were two stone feet.

'She's drugged,' said Wedge, 'to stop her making any sound. Women have coward hearts and this is dangerous work that we do.'

Jack knew his mother was brave as a fighting dog, but he said nothing.

'Right then, Jackster, hop up there, behind the carter, and away you go!'

Jack and Crispis got up on to the cart and Wedge covered them up with a horse blanket.

The driver slowly moved the pony forward and the cart left the double gates of the Dark House.

Crispis soon fell asleep to the steady sound of the hooves, and Jack, though uneasy, soon nodded off too. He had a dream. In the dream, he was standing outside a black and white timbered house of the style of grand houses that he knew. This house seemed old, although it must have been very new, and the garden was untidy. There was a sundial, and the words written round it were in Latin: TEMPUS FUGIT.

In his dream, Jack walked up to the door of the house and lifted the knocker that was in the shape of an angel. He knocked loudly, once, twice, three times . . . A girl opened the door. It was the girl in the Book of the Phoenix. It was the Golden Maiden.

Jack woke up with a start. The cart had stopped. There was no sound at all. Jack scrambled to the back of the cart – 'Mother, Mother!' But his mother was not there, only the broken legs of a broken statue.

In a panic Jack jumped clean out of the cart.

'You are returned, Jack, it is well.'

It was the Magus.

The Magus took hold of Jack the way lightning strikes a tree. One minute Jack was standing there, the next, he had been struck by a great force that seemed to go right to the centre of him. It wasn't a blow or a punch, or like being hit, it was like being caught in a storm. Jack reeled back, and fell, splintered and shaken, in the library. He had that sense that he was in a thousand pieces, and groped across the floor for his legs and arms, but in reality he was Jack, and he was the same. But he had met the power of the Magus.

'Would you still defeat me, Jack? Would you?'

Jack said nothing. The Magus was pacing the library.

'I had thought you cleverer than to trust Wedge,' said the Magus.

Jack said nothing.

'I knew that you had visited my chamber. What did

you find there, Jack?'

Jack said nothing.

The Magus reached inside his cloak and pulled out the golden casket that had contained the Egg.

'Well I know that you were searching for the Cinnabar Egg, and well I know that no man alive can open this casket unless that man is myself. Yet you betrayed me, and I warned you what would be the consequences of your betrayal.'

'Punish Wedge,' said Jack. 'He was the one who allowed me to escape.'

'He allowed nothing,' said the Magus. 'Do you yet imagine that anything happens in this house unless I allow it to happen? You did not escape. Now you shall be punished. Perhaps you had better embrace your mother – it will be for the last time.'

The Magus left the room and Jack ran into his mother's arms. She held him close, and said bravely, 'I'm not afraid, Jack. Don't you be afraid, my best boy.'

Jack said, 'Mother, whatever spell he casts will be broken when he is defeated, and his defeat is near at hand.'

Before Jack could speak further, Wedge came hopping into the room, dragging Crispis behind him.

'Jackster!' said Wedge. 'Don't go telling the Magus you gave me the Egg. He'll kill me for certain, but I'll kill this one!'

Crispis struggled to get away, but Wedge was strong.

'You betrayed me!' said Jack.

'Not that I did,' said Wedge hotly. 'I'd be glad to see the

back of you, and your mother and that dog. I said as much to Mistress Split, and SHE was the one who told tales, because of that dog! She believed that She would lose the dog! Follow you it would, She said! All lost for a dog!'

'I'll tell him about you and the Egg,' said Jack.

Wedge's face went white then green then purple. He leaned forward, his half-nose on Jack's whole nose.

'Say nothing about the Egg! Say nothing, I say! When I have power you and your own shall go free, yet if you say to Master that I have the Egg, all of us is lost!'

'I am not afraid,' said Jack.

'This one is!' said Wedge horribly. 'Look at him tremble.'

And it was true. Crispis was trembling.

Now Jack knew that he would say nothing to the Magus about the coconut he had given Wedge, because there was only one place that he, Jack, could have got the coconut, and that was from the Dragon. Jack did not want anyone except himself to start thinking about the Dragon. Tomorrow was the day when the Dragon had promised to prepare the Bath for the Sunken King. Jack knew he had to be clever. He had to duck and avoid, and let the time pass until he could free the King.

The Magus came back into the room.

'Wedge! There is no need to punish Crispis. He may go back to the other boys in the bedchamber. Leave him there and do not call him for work today. He will not be fit for the great Opus.'

Crispis didn't look at all like he would be fit for any Opus of any size. He could hardly stop his teeth chattering in his head.

Wedge let Crispis go, and the little boy fell to the floor, then scrambled up and ran off. Jack was glad. He wanted to protect Crispis, and vowed silently in his heart that Crispis would come and live with him and his mother when all this was done.

'Jack!' said the Magus. 'Did you try to bribe Wedge?'

'Yes,' said Jack, and Wedge's face went the colour of a bowl of beetroot soup, but Jack knew what to say. 'Wedge caught me searching for the Cinnabar Egg, and to avoid punishment I tried to make him help me escape.'

'And why would he help you?' said the Magus in a tone like lead.

'I said I was the only one who could get rid of the dog for him. I said that if he let me go, and Crispis, and Max and my mother, he would be happy again, because Mistress Split would not have the dog.'

'It's true, it's true!' cried Wedge. 'Didn't She betray me to keep that dog?'

And the Magus knew that this was so, and he believed the story. It was the first time that Jack had got the better of him.

'Wedge, you are a fool,' said the Magus, 'but now that this matter is clear, I shall not punish you.'

'Yes, Master. No, Master,' said Wedge, his eye gleaming with relief.

'Destroy the dog yourself if that is what you want to do.'

'No!' shouted Jack.

The Magus laughed. 'Jack, there are powerful reasons why you must quell your dislike of me and assist me in the Work. The dog is but a dog. You also have a mother. Behold!'

The Magus turned to Anne, Jack's mother.

'Anne,' said the Magus, 'did you dream one night that you were alive yet could not move at all, yet could not lift your arms nor feel your heart beating?'

'I have dreamed that dream, sir,' said Anne.

'Then dream it now,' said the Magus, and before Jack's eyes his mother's warm soft body began to harden. It had been the folds of her skirts – now it was her blouse and jacket, her strong arms that always held him when he was afraid. Anne caught her breath as she felt the cold change steal over her. Instinctively, she held out her arms, and in the position, her arms turned to stone, her arms outstretched, her palms open. The strange stone, the lifelike statue-making ceased at her neck, and Jack could see the cords of her neck throbbing as the blood still flowed there.

'Jack!' said Anne.

Jack went towards her. He touched her cold arms with his warm hands and he felt the smooth hard folds of her clothes. Then he touched her face, still warm, still full of love for him. It was as if she had heard his thoughts, and she said, 'Though my body is turned to stone, my heart is alive because of you, Jack, and, look, how my lips may still smile when I see your dear face.'

Jack stood looking at his mother, as still as stone himself.

The Magus came forward. 'You have done this, Jack. This is your disobedience. Now look carefully at your mother – once and twice she has been punished for you. The third time will be the last time and she will not speak to you again, but be as a statue in the street, and you will never know her more.'

'You said you would free her when the Work is completed!' cried Jack.

The Magus nodded. 'The power is its own power. Once, and twice, I may free her, but when she is stone and nothing but stone, then I may not free her more. Think well, Jack, think carefully what you do next. Other lives depend on you now.'

'What must I do?' asked Jack.

'You must assist me,' said the Magus. 'It is dawn. Tonight the alignment of stars and the new moon demands the beginning of the Work. In twenty-seven days' time, at the full moon, there will be an eclipse of the sun, and then the Work can be completed and the City of Gold will be mine!'

'And then?' said Jack.

'And then indeed!' repeated the Magus. 'And then your power will be no more, and you may return to the world you long for, with those you love.'

The Magus turned. 'Wedge! The boy will rest. Feed him and rest him, and secure him well. I want no further escapes – he must be ready for tonight. Do you understand?'

Wedge nodded. With his heavy hand on Jack's shoulder, he led him away.

THE DRAGON PREPARES
A BATH

The Dragon was busy.

The Dragon was the Moat and the Moat was the Dragon, but the Dragon was also not the Moat and the Moat was also not the Dragon.

Confusing.

A Dragon is a very confusing creature. But the Dragon himself is not confused.

The Dragon was busy filling the Moat with what might have been water, and was but wasn't. Not water to wash in or water to drink. This was no common or ordinary water; it was the only water in the world that could free the Sunken King.

The Dragon had this water in three enormous wooden barrels, and he carried the barrels one by one to the Moat.

He poured in the first barrel, and the Moat filled with this liquid; blue like mystery.

He poured in the second barrel and the Moat filled with that liquid; red like blood.

He poured in the third barrel and the Moat filled with a liquid that was clear like thought.

But when the three liquids from the three barrels mixed

together they made a Water that was seething, troubling, boiling black and sulphurous and stinking. This fourth Water was the Water the Dragon wanted.

The Moat was filled.

TRAPPED

Wedge had but half a brain, yet it was a brain that could work twice as hard when he wanted it to.

Wedge knew that with Jack locked up and the Magus preparing for the Opus, he would have all day to hatch the Egg and win the power for himself.

SHE would be occupied with the DOG.

He had to make sure though that Jack could not escape and Wedge knew that Jack was very good at escaping.

Wedge mused on Jack's capacity to escape, and reasoned it thus: 'If there is a door, then Jackster opens it. If there is a lock, then Jackster springs it. If I imprison him where there is neither lock nor door, then escape he cannot.'

And with that in mind, or half in mind, Wedge marched Jack into the kitchen and opened a hatch in the wall, where there was a small sturdy platform hanging by four ropes.

'Pull yourself up, Jackster!' said Wedge. 'Go on with it!'

Reluctantly, Jack began to pull. Up he went, up and up and up and up and up and up and up and up and up and up and up and up and up until he thought his arms would break.

At the last second of his strength, he tumbled out through a second hatch, into a small sealed turret room. There was a window but there was no door.

Down below, Wedge deftly released the ropes that secured the pulley, and the platform shot back down, fast and furious, and Jack, panting and staring down the shaft, saw that there was no way out.

He heard Wedge's voice, faint and far off. 'The Magus will come for you, Jackster, never fear!'

Below, below, Jack heard the faint hop-hop of Wedge departing. He looked around him.

The turret room was comfortable and furnished. Once upon a time someone had used this room for sleeping – there was a small heavy bed by the wall; and for reading – the round walls were lined with books. An armchair had been placed by the window, but the wood was wormy and the leather had long since dried and torn away. No one had been here for a very long time.

Jack looked out of the window. In the nest of the Phoenix he had been high up, at the top of the house, or so he had thought, but here was so high that the clouds floated in through the window like white smoke, and only sometimes, when the wind blew them away, could he see anything below.

Below was much below, another country called Below. The Thames was so far underneath his gaze that it looked like a silver thread drawn through a dark cloth, and not like a mighty river at all.

He could not climb down and he could not use his iron tool because there was no door, or if there was a door it was not one that Jack could find by any ordinary investigation.

He leaned sadly out of the window.

And that was when he saw someone else leaning sadly out of the window two turrets away. It was a girl. It was the girl in the Book of the Phoenix.

DOG DOES IT AGAIN!

I n the kitchen, Max slid out from his hiding place behind the woodpile, and seeing that Mistress Split was still snoring on her truckle bed, he used his paw to pull open the heavy kitchen door and set off by himself through the Dark House. He was a dog. He knew where he was going.

First, Max slid like a silent shadow into the library and ran to Jack's mother, and jumped up on the table so that he could lick her nose.

'Max!' said Anne. 'Do you know where they have imprisoned Jack?' Max wagged his tail, and jumping down, he went softly to the door into the laboratory, where his quick ears could hear the Magus giving orders to the boys to chop and fire and stoke and fill.

Then, turning his friendly intelligent face to Anne, to reassure her, Max set off again through the house.

He went up the stairs and put his nose round the half-door of the Creature's chamber. Sure enough, there was Wedge, with the coconut in front of him, and a very large hen.

Max ran at top speed up the turning stairs until he came to the boys' chamber, where he knew he would find Crispis.

Yes, there he was, sitting disconsolately on the edge of his stone bed, swinging his thin legs. He was talking to a flower pot, where, just starting to grow, was a sunflower.

Max barked and Crispis got up and came over to pat the dog. 'Where's Jack?' asked Crispis. 'I wish I was an all-seeing eye so that I could find him.'

But Max was an all-smelling nose, and he knew where Jack was, and he wanted to show Crispis. Tugging at the boy's jacket, running a few feet, then tugging again, Max made Crispis understand he had to follow him.

Crispis was quite frightened to be leaving the chamber without permission, but then, he thought, he was usually frightened, whatever was happening, so this was probably all right. But he took his sunflower just in case.

Down they went, creeping past the Creature's chamber, and in one brief half a second half a glance, Crispis saw Wedge on top of a large brown hen and the hen on top of a small brown coconut.

THE TRUTH ABOUT SUNFLOWERS

'What's your name?' called Jack to the girl, but every time the girl replied, her answer was caught by the windy clouds and carried away.

But Jack knew she was the Captive.

And he knew she was the Golden Maiden.

But he wanted to know her name.

In the laboratory, the Magus had made ready. The fearful heat of the furnace had caused some of the boys to faint, and Robert was reviving William and Anselm with water. The two giant alembics bubbled and boiled and filled with steam. The Magus ran from one to another, drawing off a silver liquid that immediately hardened into a solid silver ball. Yet when William dropped one of these small round balls it splintered into a thousand tiny replicas of itself, like ball bearings.

The Magus cursed, and sent the boys on their hands and knees to find and collect the tiny drops of mercury.

'The Spirit Mercurius is essential to the Work,' shouted the Magus over the boom and boil of the alembics. 'Lose no part of him, for he is liquid and solid, matter and mind.'

Round and round the laboratory swooped and dived the

Eyebat, but often it threw itself at the skylight, making chattering noises, like a cat when it sees a bird.

And beyond the laboratory, silent and motionless as ever, were the stone boys.

'Make ready,' said the Magus, 'and leave me. The Work is begun . . .'

And the Sunken King turning and turning in his tank like a child in its mother's womb.

And the Dragon that held the Cinnabar Egg like a world that holds a star.

And the Dark House waiting like a baleful thought.

And now, and now, and now.

'Woof,' barked Max at the foot of the shaft. 'Woof. Woof, Woof.'

Up above Jack heard, and ran from the window and looked down. But it was such a long way down.

'What are we going to do?' said Crispis. 'I wish I was a bird and then I could rescue him.'

Crispis sighed and put down his sunflower, in its pot, on the floor, in the shaft. Then, for no reason that he understood, he went to the vast stone sink that stood in the kitchen, and drew off a jug of water from the water barrel kept beneath. Mistress Split snored on.

Crispis went back to his sunflower and watered it. And it grew – about two feet, all at once.

'Oh!' said Crispis. And he watered it once more, and it grew another two feet, and now it had begun to grow its way up into the shaft and up it went, and up it went and up and up and up and up and up and up and up and up.

And Jack suddenly realised that something was coming towards him, and he stood back, and watched, amazed as the sunflower grew into the room.

But it did not stop when it reached the room. What the sunflower did was this: it grew over towards the window, and then and only then, when its top was in the fresh air and the white clouds, did it stop growing.

And then, like the sun itself, the sunflower sprung a great golden head and shone so bright from the window, that a woman polishing a copper pot in the street miles below, saw the light of it beaming, and looked up. 'Lord,' she said, 'the sun so visible, twice in the sky at once! Certainly strange happenings there must be in some place.'

And she hurried inside.

Jack didn't hesitate. Testing the sturdy stem of the plant just once, he shinned right down it at such a speed that his head went dizzy, and in a few seconds: there he was. Landed in the kitchen on his bottom, and Max standing on him and licking every bit of him and Crispis dancing for joy.

'It was the Dragon's sunflower!' he said.

Jack felt in his pocket and gave Crispis another of the six

remaining seeds. 'Keep it safe in case you need it again,' he said, and Crispis nodded solemnly and stowed the seed away in his stocking top.

The boys were just tiptoeing across the kitchen when Mistress Split woke up with a vast yawn. There was half a pause of hesitation, then Max bounded into her arm, and in the bounding and the 'Boojie Boojie Boojie!' that took up the next half minute, Jack and Crispis slipped out of the door.

'Where's Wedge?' whispered Jack.

'He's trying to hatch the coconut you gave him. He's got a hen the size of a pig,' said Crispis.

Jack smiled and nodded. Now they had a chance.

Light and silent, the two boys went straight into the cellar.

THE BATH OF SULPHUR

There was the Sunken King, now so faint a presence that he could hardly be seen dissolving in the water.

'It's time!' said Jack. 'You must come with us now.'

The Sunken King turned his face, and Jack could hardly hear him as he spoke.

'Pull the plug, Adam Kadmon, but know that I shall die very soon if what you say is untrue. Once outside of this place I have but a short time.'

The plug . . . Jack searched frantically around until he found what looked like a plug in the side of the tank. With all his strength he turned it and pulled it but it was stuck fast.

He heard a familiar voice, like fire rolling down a mountain.

'How so, Jack Snap, how so? Are you not here yet? I am ready. I am here.'

Jack walked round to the back of the tank. The whole wall of the cellar had been demolished, and in place of the wall, like a wall, but not a wall, was the Dragon himself.

'Bring him to me, Jack. The Bath is prepared.'

'I can't pull the plug!' said Jack desperately. 'Will you help me?'

'That was not part of our bargain,' said the Dragon. 'You must come or not come.'

Jack nearly yelled at the Dragon, but he stopped himself and his anger. The Magus . . . anger . . . if Jack felt anger or fear he would betray himself to the Magus like everyone who had come before him, like everyone in the Dark House.

Jack looked around the damp bare cellar. Then, without a question or a hesitation, he ripped the flare from its bracket on the wall and swung it with every ounce of his strength at the glass tank.

CRASH!

He swung again, and again, using both arms, his arms and shoulders taut.

CRASH!

The tank shattered into pieces and the water flowed out in a deluge. Jack thought he would be drowned, but the moment the water escaped the tank, it was not water at all, but something silver and shining and it seemed to disappear. Whatever it was, it wasn't wet.

Jack ran forward into the shattered tank and bent to pick up the Sunken King, who was light as a bone, and white as a bleached bone.

Jack had the King across his shoulders, and he carried him, weightless like a bird, and he stepped forward, out through the cellar and to the moat.

Where the Dragon was waiting.

'How now, Jack Snap. Into the moat with him, for that is your Bath.'

The smell was overpowering – like rotten meat and horse dung and dead rats.

Jack looked into the moat. He was horrified. This was no bath, this was a boiling, bubbling, seething mass of black mud and filth. The King would be killed.

'It's a trick!' shouted Jack. 'You have tricked me!'

And suddenly Jack saw himself standing alone, bearing a burden that, light as it was, he could not carry, charged with a task it was impossible to complete, confused by other people, without help. A boy, he was just a boy, twelve years old, and in front of him was a dragon who had hatched inside time as though time itself were an egg, and here was the Dragon, ancient and wily . . .

Jack lost heart.

And in the moment that he lost heart, the Magus in the laboratory sprang to his feet, and with a rush and a roar, it was as a phoenix that he flew, flew, flew, from the upper sky-light, now circling over the moat, fierce and dark and massive.

'Throw the King, Jack Snap!' the Dragon spoke.

'Adam Kadmon, obey!' It was the feeble voice of the King speaking, and hardly knowing what he did, Jack threw the King, who seemed to be made of white feathers and hollow bones, into the moat.

The Phoenix made a dive, and Jack ducked just in time to avoid its beak, but its cruel golden feet caught his arm as he folded his arms over his head for protection. Jack felt as though he had been burned.

As the Phoenix made its fearful arc in the sky, Jack looked

into the moat and saw the Sunken King desperately flailing his arms and crying for help. By now, he was covered in black filth, and hardly visible.

He's drowning, thought Jack, and then he didn't think at all, took the biggest breath of air he could, and flung himself into the stinking stench.

Jack sank. The slurry in the moat was thick and sucking, like quicksand. It was all his nightmares, all his fears, and it was black without end.

Jack swept his arms about blindly, and found the King. He pulled the King to him so that they were one body, arms and legs wrapped around each other, and with all his strength, Jack kicked up, trying to bring them into the air.

And then a very strange thing happened.

As Jack's head split the gluey surface of the moat, the Sunken King smiled at him. And Jack saw the face of a young man, a strong man, with clean red hair, like a sun.

The thin body Jack held against his grew stronger and fatter; he could feel real legs and real arms, and he had the sensation that these real legs and real arms were his own legs and arms. He held the King, only their heads above the moat.

'Adam Kadmon,' said the King. 'That is our name. Take my ring.' And he pulled a ring from his finger and placed it on Jack's finger.

The moat began to change. First its texture thinned from thick to running. Then its colour changed from black to clear, and Jack looked down, and it was as though he was in a running river with nothing to hide. Fish swam.

'The Phoenix and the Fishes,' said the King, 'the Tree and the Wind that blows in the Tree.'

Jack didn't understand, but these were the last words of the Sunken King, for he began to dissolve, not as he had in the tank, in formless despair, but because he was becoming something else. And the something else he was becoming was Jack.

Jack was alone in the clear shining water. He swam to the edge and hauled himself out. The water ran from him in silver showers, and in the puddles it made were balls of silver. The King's ring on his own finger flashed and caught the sun.

'How now, Jack Snap,' said the Dragon.

'What has happened?' asked Jack.

'You have absorbed the powers of the old King,' said the Dragon, 'because you are the Radiant Boy, the one who is to come.'

'To come where?' said Jack. 'I don't understand.'

The Dragon flicked its purple tongue. 'Understanding will follow. But first you must become what you are.'

There was a rush of flaming wings. The Phoenix landed right in front of Jack, its eyes like rubies, its wing-feathers flames.

The Phoenix spoke. 'You found the Cinnabar Egg and you freed the Sunken King. I underestimated you, Jack Snap. Now you cannot be my assistant, for you have become my rival.'

'I want nothing to do with you,' said Jack. 'I want to leave this place for ever.'

'It is too late for that,' replied the Phoenix. 'You have chosen.'

'That is so, Jack Snap,' said the Dragon. 'You have chosen.'

'Now one of us shall defeat the other,' said the Phoenix, 'and the one who is defeated shall never live again. Do you accept this challenge?'

'No!' said Jack.

The sky was dark and thundery. The Dragon was purple and green. The Phoenix was red and gold. Jack was as silver as the silver water in the moat.

He heard a voice he knew, yet didn't know, saying his name.

He turned round. It was the girl from the tower. The Golden Maiden. The Captive. She was wearing strange clothes that he had never seen before, but her face was not strange, it was strangely familiar.

'Jack! You have to accept the task that is given to you.'

And Jack remembered again the story of Arthur and the sword in the stone, and he remembered the stone boys, and his mother, already half-stone, and this stone house, heavy, imprisoned. Something had to be set free, some better power than the one that ruled this house now.

Jack looked at the girl under the thundery sky. She was smiling, but her eyes were serious, as serious as stars.

He turned to the Phoenix. 'Yes,' he said, 'I will, and yes.'

THE NIGREDO

There was a shudder and a shimmer, and all at once the Phoenix had vanished, and in its place stood the Magus in his long black cloak. He was holding a big iron key.

'Jack, the doors to the Dark House are open now. I can no longer prevent your coming and going. You are your own master now. But follow me, if you please – this one last time . . .'

Jack was confused. The Magus was his enemy. Why was his enemy talking like a friend?

Jack followed the Magus into the house and into the laboratory. There was a vessel on the floor sealed and wrapped in sacking. Some of the smaller tongs and bellows and stirrers and jars were packed in cases. Wedge was there, frantically wrapping and stacking.

Then Jack saw his mother. She had been carried into the laboratory.

'I was about to put her with the other statues,' said the Magus, 'but as she is your mother, you may decide for yourself.'

'She is not stone,' said Jack, a cold fear creeping through him.

'Is she not?' replied the Magus mildly, and then he

grabbed Jack's arm, and pulled him to the brazier that leapt with green flames. Jack realised that his own physical strength had greatly increased, and that he could throw off the Magus if he chose to, but because he was afraid, he did not do so.

'Jack,' said the Magus, 'how different it might have been if you had served me. Together we could have ruled the City of Gold and, piece by piece, land by land, the whole world. You as my rightful heir.'

'You have a son,' said Jack. 'His name is William.'

The face of the Magus darkened like a lake at night. 'I have no son. He failed me. He could not complete the Work. There he is – with the rest.'

Jack shook the Magus off him, and walked into the antechamber beyond the laboratory. He shuddered. All the boys were there now: Anselm, Robert, William, Peter, Roderick . . .

'Crispis . . .' he said under his breath, but the child was so small he could not see if he was there or not.

'Why have you done this?' said Jack, angry.

'They are of no further use,' replied the Magus.

Jack walked sadly towards the statues and put his hand on Robert's shoulder. His heart was burning with sadness and anger, but he knew he must show nothing to the Magus. He was not ready yet to test his power.

The Magus was timing the progress of the moon. He smiled his dark smile. 'And now,' he said, 'I will give you a free choice, Jack, for you are not my servant but my enemy, yet because you have taken the power of the Sunken King, and because you are the Radiant Boy, I must bargain with you. Here is my bargain. Put your hand in the fire with mine, as the new moon aligns with Mars, and your mother goes free. If you do not . . .'

'My hand in the fire?' asked Jack, who was afraid, not of the pain, but of the true motives of the Magus.

'I must join with you to use your power,' said the Magus. 'Only the golden power of the Radiant Boy can complete the Work.'

'No!' said Jack. 'I will not do it.'

The Magus glanced out of the window. There was the moon. 'Then . . .' said the Magus.

Jack returned to the laboratory and looked at his mother. As he looked, a hard grey cold began to steal over those warm parts of her that yet remained. He saw her lips half open in surprise, his own half-name just issuing from them like a whisper. Then the air in her nose seemed to freeze. Her eyes implored him. Jack grabbed the Magus by the arm, and with easy power – and he saw the surprise in the Magus's face – Jack plunged their twined arms into the flames.

The flames leapt up, like snakes, like coils of dark life, for the fire was no ordinary fire, and its brightness was dark, and in truth its heat was dread cold.

All the time that their arms burned, Jack kept his eyes fixed on the Magus, and he saw in those eyes many lives, many secrets, and he thought he saw one single fear. If he could find that fear . . .

The fire burned down and went out. The brazier was void and cool. Jack stood back, shaking his arm, which seemed just as it had been. The Magus nodded his head.

'Thank you, Jack. You served me after all.'

Then, with a rush of wind, the Magus was gone.

Jack went to his mother. He stroked her hair, but it was stone. He touched her cheek, but it was hard. He kissed her lips, but they were cold. She was motionless and still.

He betrayed me, thought Jack bitterly. *I gave him my power, and he betrayed me.*

Jack looked around the laboratory. The furnaces were out and the alembics no longer bubbled and popped.

He walked through into the library. The books had gone. The stone shelves were empty. He walked through into the hall – and the place was hung with silence.

A great weight at his heart, and darkness all around him, Jack sat down on the floor. He did not know what to do.

In all his life he had never felt so desolate or so desperate. He loved his mother, and now he had lost her. The Magus was free and powerful. He, Jack, had ruined it all.

'Please come back,' he said to himself in a whisper. 'Mother, please come back.'

He felt something small and warm against his legs. It was Max come to find him. Max licked him and leaned against him, making small noises of encouragement. Jack stroked the dog, but he was too numb to do anything more. He felt as though he had been turned to stone himself.

SOME LIGHT

'Jack?'

Jack looked up from his long silence. He did not know how much time had passed. The night seemed to be the day now, but what day?

The girl from the tower was squatting near him.

'You are the Golden Maiden,' said Jack. 'You escaped from the tower . . .'

'Well. I realised that no one was going to rescue me,' said the girl. 'I mean, that only happens in fairy stories, doesn't it? So I rescued myself. Well, that isn't strictly true. The sunflower grew out of your window and across into my window, and I climbed across it, and then all the way down, like you did, into the kitchen. Then the dog came and fetched me, just like he did now.'

Max came up, wagging his tail and wanting to be stroked.

'The dog's called Max,' said Jack.

'And you are Jack . . .' said the girl.

'And what's your name?'

'Silver,' said Silver.

'That's strange, when you are the Golden Maiden . . .'

'Who says I'm the Golden Maiden?' asked Silver.

'The Book of the Phoenix,' said Jack simply. 'I saw your

picture, and then I thought I was knocking at the door of a house, and that you answered.'

'You were,' said Silver. 'I did. That's how I got here, because you were calling me, and I came through the fire.'

'What fire?' asked Jack.

And Silver explained how she had walked through the fire in the library at home, and reappeared in the library of the Magus.

'Do you know the Magus?'

'No, but I know he's an alchemist, and the last alchemist I met wanted to control time – all of it. It was to do with a clock . . .'

'The Magus is an alchemist, yes,' said Jack, 'and he wants to turn all the city of London into gold – every bit of it.'

'They always want every bit – all of the gold, all of the time,' said Silver. 'Mine had to be defeated, and yours will have to be defeated too. I suppose I've got to help.'

'Where do you come from?' asked Jack. 'Why do you wear those strange clothes? What are they made from?'

Silver looked at her jeans and fleece and trainers. 'I come from Cheshire, in England. It's in the north of England. And this is London in England, isn't it?'

'Yes,' said Jack, 'and Elizabeth is Queen.'

'What year is it?' asked Silver.

'1601,' said Jack, looking doubtfully at Silver. 'You should know that.'

'I'm not from your time, Jack,' said Silver. 'That's why I wear these clothes. I come from the twenty-first century.'

Jack didn't speak. He just gazed at Silver, his brow furrowed. He felt tired and muddled. Nothing made sense . . . the Sunken King, the Dragon, the Moat, the Magus, his mother, his mother, his mother. That was the dull ache in his body, his mother . . .

He got up. 'The Dragon might know . . .' he said, not knowing what he meant. Silver followed him.

They walked through the empty house. All the doors always so carefully closed and locked were open. It was as though a great wind had blown through the house. The library was empty of books, the door to the laboratory stood ajar on its heavy hinges. The door to the downward tree and the Dragon's lair was gone altogether, and of the tree and the deep forest, there was no sign. The Dragon had gone, and taken his forest with him.

Jack went upstairs; Wedge's half-room was half empty, half packed half not packed, like someone running away in a hurry.

The boys' bedchamber was as usual, with the seven stone beds in their stony line, but it felt like years since anyone had been there. The whole house felt like it had been empty for years, echoing sounds and damp smells and a chilly neglect. Jack pointed up through the ceiling, to where he had found the nest of the Phoenix and the Cinnabar Egg.

Jack suddenly slipped and fell, and Silver could see that the boy was dizzy with exhaustion. She led him into the boys' bedchamber and plumped up a bed for him as best she could, using all the blankets and pillows. While she was doing this, Jack was staring at the King's ring on his finger. He tried to take it off but he couldn't shift it.

'I have to go to sleep,' he said wearily, 'and when I wake up, Golden Maiden, tell me all this has never been.'

Jack fell asleep at once, and Max lay down at his feet, with one eye open, black and shining like a living coal.

Silver stood for a moment. She realised she was cold. She looked around for a blanket, realised she had piled them all on Jack, then noticed some clothes belonging to the other boys. It occurred to her that she would be the only person in Elizabethan England wearing jeans, trainers and a fleece. Time for a change . . .

She found woollen breeches, a thick coarse shirt, a leather jerkin, a cap, flat leather shoes and stockings. The stockings were a bit smelly so she decided to keep on her own long socks that were made of wool anyway, because although she came from the future, her house had been built in the past, and it was always freezing. *If this is 1601*, she thought, *the house I live in is only thirteen years old! If I could go there now, it would be new . . . But it would still be freezing.*

She pulled on her cap, shoving her unruly curly red hair out of the way. If no one inspected her too closely, she could be a young boy – like Jack.

She went over to the window and looked out at the skyline of spires and fires. Smoke from the tall chimneys billowed everywhere. This wooden London was all fires and churches, it seemed to her; and she remembered from her history books that before the Great Fire in 1666, London was like a forest, a vast seething growing forest, made out of people and wood – buildings of wood, and burnings of wood. Far past the tight lines of the city were open fields. And Silver thought how it would be, over four hundred years later, of glass and concrete, of cars and buses. How unlikely. How impossible . . .

Breaking her thoughts, Silver went on to the landing. She was drawn to the attic space that Jack had shown her – the nest of the Phoenix. She was agile and strong and light, and by balancing on the banister rail, she could just reach into the opening, and then she pulled herself up, crossing her feet, lifting her knees, and propelling herself through the gap. She fell flat on her face and almost choked with the feathers.

She got up and dusted herself down, her eyes getting used to the dim light. She saw the heavy carved desk, and the book on the desk.

The Book of the Phoenix! she thought.

Silver went over to it. It was open at the page of the Radiant Boy – and there was Jack.

She turned the page – the Golden Maiden. Yes, there she was. Herself. And she was holding her emblem – the clock known as the Timekeeper.

But Jack won't know anything about that, thought Silver.

Now Silver was an ordinary girl, and an extraordinary girl, all at the same time, and this wasn't her first strange adventure – *but Jack won't know anything about that*, she said to herself again, wondering what to tell him, how much to explain . . .

She looked curiously through the pages, and most of it she couldn't read because it was in Latin, but she could see that it was a book about alchemy. There were the alembics, and there was the Nigredo – that was the black sludge stuff that had filled up the Moat – and there was the Phoenix, and there was the Dragon, and there was the spirit mercurius, or mercury, quicksilver and strange. Yes, she knew quite a lot about alchemy, thanks to . . . She shuddered. She didn't want to think about him.

For a long time Silver sat reading and trying to read the book. Then she noticed it was getting dark, and that the whole day must have passed. *A short day*, she thought, but then she knew from past experience that some days are shorter than others, that time is not what it seems to be by the sun and the clock . . .

She would go and wake Jack, and they would decide what to do next. Silver decided to take the Book of the Phoenix with her, but she couldn't swing herself down carrying it, and she didn't want to just drop it through the floor. She looked around. There was an old disused bell-pull in the room, of the kind you use when you ring for a servant, and Silver thought she could take down the bell-pull, tie the cord round the book, and lower the book down on to the landing.

She gave a great tug at the frayed cord, but as it tore from its hook, a bell began to ring, *clang clang clang* – and on it went, *clang clang clang*, even though Silver was no longer pulling the cord.

Quickly she did as she had planned, lowered and dropped the book, then swung herself down after it.

Clang clang clang! Clang clang clang!

The bell woke up Jack.

Max, whose ears were sharper and faster than those of his human friends, began barking. Far below, from somewhere so far below it might have been the bowels of the earth, came a clanking noise, as though an engine or a rusty machine were beginning to grind and whirr.

Silver ran towards Jack, who came stumbling sleepily out of the bedchamber. The two of them gazed down over the banister rail. Max stuck his head between the stair rods, because like it or not, ready or not, someone, something, was coming up the stairs.

THE KNIGHT
SUMMONED

J ack and Silver could see his helmet. They could see his breast plate, his greaves, his iron feet. By his side was a long sword in a blue scabbard, and his hands were protected by chain-mail gloves.

The Knight did not hurry, nor did he pause. Nor did he speak, nor give any sign. He turned the final stairs and stood before Jack and Silver. He did not speak.

Then he kneeled down, and raised his visor. His eyes were deep and black.

'I am the Knight Summoned,' he said. 'My name is Sir Boris of the Golden Bell.'

'I didn't mean to summon you,' said Silver. 'I didn't know the bell was still working.'

'The bell is the bell,' said the Knight, and Silver thought this very enigmatic and difficult to follow, but she did not feel she could argue with a knight in shining armour.

'Now that you are summoned,' said Silver, 'what happens next?'

'I shall travel with you,' said the Knight, 'as your Knight, waiting upon the hour when I shall know what is to be known.'

Silver realised that talking to the Knight might be a

challenge. 'Thank you,' she said, and looked at Jack.

The Knight stood to his feet. He was about seven feet tall.

Jack was slowly coming to his senses. He had been through a great ordeal, and it had forced him into a kind of trance. When he had slept he had dreamed that his mother had come to him, begging him to free her. He had woken at the sound of the bell, with his hand clutching the hard stone of the bed.

'We must leave this place,' he said, and once again, as when he had spoken to the Dragon, he had a feeling of something else speaking through him – a kind of knowledge that he did not yet understand.

'But where are we going?' asked Silver. 'I mean, we've got to sleep somewhere.'

Jack didn't answer. He couldn't answer. Yet he knew what was to be done. He went down the stairs, Silver and Max following him, and behind them all, the heavy steady iron tread of the Knight.

Jack showed the Knight the stone boys in the antechamber behind the laboratory, and asked Sir Boris if he could carry them into the courtyard and load them on to a cart. But Jack said nothing about his mother.

'Jack, we can't leave if we have nowhere to go,' said Silver, who wondered if Jack was all right in the head.

'We cannot stay if we have nowhere to stay,' said Jack. 'This house is no more.'

Silver was hungry, and had been hoping to find something

to eat before they set off.

'And I must find the Magus,' said Jack.

As Jack spoke he heard a familiar voice.

'How so, Jack Snap, how so?'

It was the Dragon.

The Dragon was looking in through the window of the laboratory. His eyes were ancient and wily, yet not cruel.

'You have summoned the Knight,' said the Dragon.

'That was me,' said Silver, 'and it was a mistake.'

The Dragon regarded her. 'Girl with the Golden Face, what comes to pass is what comes to pass.'

Silver wondered if everyone she was going to meet was going to talk like this. The Knight clanked by, carrying Anselm made of stone.

'The Knight will fight me,' said the Dragon, 'when it is time.'

The Knight clanked by, carrying William.

'He hasn't even noticed you,' said Silver, 'which is amazing as you are a dragon, and your head is enormous, and poking through a very small window.'

'Until it is time it is not time,' said the Dragon, with an air of finality. 'Until it is time we shall not meet again. Jack Snap, thank you for the Egg.'

'What is inside the Cinnabar Egg?' asked Jack.

'I am,' said the Dragon.

'Huh?' said Silver, who was really wishing she was back home in bed.

'And not only I. A mystery, and how so, Jack Snap!'

And then the Dragon withdrew his head, and there began very quietly at first, and then not quietly at all, a deep shaking, like an earthquake, like the ground was ripping.

'Look out!' cried Silver, as a piece of masonry fell right in between them.

Silver thought that the bulk of the Dragon had dislodged part of the roof, but Jack knew better.

'All speed!' he cried. 'The house is demolishing itself!'

Jack shook himself like a dog shakes itself after a plunge in the water. He was suddenly fully awake, fully alert. The stupor and sadness fell from him, and he felt great strength and purpose. Not knowing how he did it, hardly noticing that he did it, he picked up the stone statue that was his mother and ran with it from the room.

Silver got out of the laboratory just as the ceiling came crashing to the floor. She had the Book of the Phoenix under her arm, and pelted as fast as her legs could carry her as the walls of the house started to split and groan.

In the courtyard, Jack and Max were already up on the cart, the statues laid behind, and the Knight ready beside them on a beautiful grey horse.

Then they heard a cry – 'HELP! HELP!'

At that moment the whole side wall of the house began to crumble and collapse. Jack looked around wildly, trying to see where the voice came from.

It was Crispis, waving from behind a small barred window two floors up.

'I have to save him!' cried Jack. 'Take the cart, go on, go on!'

Crispis had hidden himself from the Dragon, from the Magus, from Wedge, from Mistress Split, from the whole world, by shutting himself into a cupboard where he sometimes shut himself to be quiet, and so he had saved himself from being turned into stone.

But he had fallen asleep, and when he awoke, he had been hungry, so he had eaten the second of the sunflower seeds that Jack had given to him – and a very strange thing had happened – he had turned bright yellow.

As Jack ran back to the crumbling destroying house, he remembered what Robert had said about the house being a kind of thought – that it didn't really exist. Then the Magus was 'unthinking' the house, and the house in its volcanic shudders was trying to throw off all the weight of matter, and return again to an idea or a dream. The Magus had made it, now he could unmake it. But it was still heavy, still solid, and there was nothing dreamlike about the lead gutters and stone tiles flying like deadly missiles at Jack's head.

A side stair was already standing on its own, its walls fallen away. Jack leapt up the staircase two treads at a time, following the cries of Crispis, until he came to the cupboard jammed shut by a fallen gargoyle.

Jack was strong now, and he threw the grinning stone gargoyle imp aside, and pulled his small friend free. Over his shoulder Crispis dangled, and Jack ran again, in zigzags, jumping, ducking, leaping, as the house crumbled and collapsed into the moat.

1601

S ilver had never driven a horse and cart in her life, but she took the reins, and the horse seemed to know how to go forward, and forward they went, out through the court-yard and into Dark House Lane and down towards the River Thames.

Stables, kennels, breweries, carpenters' shops, pudding dens, places where they stitched jerkins, made tallow candles, forged horses' hooves, inns, taverns, bakers, cookshops, men and women with fish baskets on their heads, men and women alike smoking short clay pipes, dogs running in and out of cartwheels, a parrot on a perch shouting at passers-by, a woman selling bolts of cloth from a handcart, a tinker with pots and pans hung round his thin body, a fiddler playing a melody, a sheep in the middle of the pitted lane, the smell of cooking, a pork smell, like roasting, and a smell like iron being heated so that it glowed. A little boy with bare feet, a girl carrying a baby, a donkey with a man on its back – a man so tall that his feet tripped along the ground as the donkey plodded on. Two soldiers, ragged and frightening, waved their fists at Silver, but she was brave, and urged the horse and cart on.

Then she came towards the river.

The River Thames, wide like in a dream – jammed with craft and bodies, like in a nightmare.

Black boats that were the charcoal burners. Boats tarred and blistering in the sun. Boats smothered in pitch to keep the water out. Boats sanded and oiled and curtained and secret to keep out prying eyes. Rich boats like these, and poor boats like the others. Boats that carried barrels of beer, and boats half sunk under the weight of cattle, mooing and lowing at the slopping water.

There were naval boats, proud in blue and gold, and merchant boats with their Guild insignia embossed into the prow. There were scavenger boats trawling their nets to drag up what others had lost, and gaily painted boats carrying visitors to and fro. There was a boat full of cats – so full of cats that the boat itself looked to be made out of fur. These were ships' cats coming ashore or going to sail, a mewling, rioting, spitting, sunning, tails-in-the-air-legs-akimbo of a boat, so noisy that a sloop packed with priests had their fingers in their ears, and the drunken party-goers sailing nearby nearly fell overboard for laughing.

And this was London. And this was the life of London. And this was the life of London rolled out like a carpet and played like a tune, and smelling to high heaven of fish and meat and animals and dung and sweat and beer and the hot scorching acrid smells of leather tanners and blacksmiths, and the steam and hiss of water and flesh as the cattle were branded on the stumpy piers.

London, thought Silver. *1601*.

And then there was a figure running beside her, strong and fast and covered in thick, damp, dirty, chalky dust. In his arms he carried the smallest possible child, also covered in dust, but this child, no mistaking it, was bright yellow, except for his halo of curly hair, which was now jet black. The child looked exactly like a sunflower.

'Crispis!' panted Jack, flinging the child up into the cart, and hopping up himself. 'Turn right here, Mistress Silver, if you don't want to end up in the river!'

As Jack took over the reins of the cart, and they swung off along the river towards the Strand, Jack had a feeling of being watched.

He looked up into the sky. Hovering, swooping, dipping, diving, shearing the clouds and grazing the spires, free at last and exulting and malevolent, two eyes glared down. It was the Eyebat.

Instinctively Jack looked out on to the teeming river, and sure enough, he saw what he saw.

Quite on its own, in the hugger-mugger of craft, was a golden boat. It was a dark gold, not a shining gold, but gold it was, and quite different to the other vessels plying their way.

Jack recognised Wedge, and Mistress Split, each rowing a single oar, with their single arm. Standing in the prow, wrapped in black, was the Magus.

'He's here,' said Jack.

'Of course he's here,' answered Silver, narrowing her eyes

213

across the waterline. 'This is the doing that you have to do,' and then she realised that she was sounding as peculiar and enigmatic as the Dragon or the Knight.

She looked again. A second boat was approaching that of the Magus. And the person rowing it . . . no, it couldn't be him. Silver stared and stared. It couldn't be . . .

'What can you see?' asked Jack. But Silver shook her head and didn't answer. She was looking at someone from another time . . .

The bells were ringing twelve noon.

'I think we should visit Mother Midnight,' said Jack.

MORE MOTHER
MIDNIGHT

I t was just as before, though nothing in this life ever is just as before, and the repeats, however similar, are not identical; the tiny difference between two moments holds the clue.

She had been there for centuries, it seemed, under the canopy of the oak, living in the roots of the oak, burning her mysterious fire that needed no fuel yet roared red.

What a figure the woman was – so small she could have lived in a box. So thin that she could have escaped from a hole in a box. Her mouth was as empty as an empty box, and her eyes were as full of secrets as a box that says DO NOT OPEN. She was not a human, not a fish, not a cat, not a dog, not a monster, not a devil, not a born thing, not anything. She was all manner of things. She was Mother Midnight.

Jack and Silver went down the low corridor and sat at the table that was made from the tree. There was the copper bowl filled with green water.

'You must pay me,' said Mother Midnight, but Jack had no money.

'What have you in your pockets?' she said, and Jack turned out nothing but the five remaining sunflower seeds.

Mother Midnight stretched out her leathery palm. 'The

price is two,' she said, and Jack gave them to her.

'I will help you,' said Mother Midnight, 'but bring in the yellow child from the cart. There is always danger.'

Jack went to get Crispis. Mother Midnight stared at Silver.

'I know you,' said Mother Midnight. 'You are old.'

'I am thirteen,' said Silver, 'and I don't know you.'

Mother Midnight laughed. 'You, you have been alive and you will be alive again.'

Silver didn't like the sound of this. 'I am alive now,' she said.

Mother Midnight shook her head. 'Yet not in this time. In this time you are but a visitor from another time.'

'Yes,' said Silver. 'Who called me?'

'The Radiant Boy calls the Golden Maiden.'

'Is that why I am here?' asked Silver. 'It's just that, on the river, I saw . . . thought I saw, might have seen –'

But before she could speak further, Jack came back with Crispis. The yellow boy sat down by the red-eyed cat.

'My mother has been turned to stone!' said Jack.

Mother Midnight nodded. 'The power you do possess that can free her body from the stone, but you must break the power of the Magus, and from that victory all else shall follow.'

'How am I to defeat him? He has cheated me of my power already!'

'Power you have, and it will grow as you use it. Are you not strong in body? Stronger than any man?'

218

Jack thought of lifting the stone statue of his mother, and rescuing Crispis. He nodded.

Mother Midnight nodded. 'Now you will learn how to be strong in spirit. Then you will defeat him.'

'There isn't time!' said Jack. 'He's in the city, he took my power, he turned my mother to stone, he's going to turn the whole city into gold!'

Mother Midnight held up her gnarled hand. 'Be calm! Follow the time and you will know the time – this girl, the Golden Maiden, will be your timekeeper. She will tell you when what must begin will begin.'

'Riddles, all riddles!' cried Jack. 'The Magus, the Dragon, you . . .'

And he stood up, agitated and angry. He wanted someone to tell him what to do and how to do it.

'You will see me again,' said Mother Midnight, 'but now, get gone!'

The fire roared up. The cat jumped on to the shoulders of his eerie mistress and Jack and Silver and Crispis crept out of the low den and into the bustle of the alley.

THE ANCESTOR

J ack turned the cart, and travelling slowly, without speaking, they came to the house on the Strand called The Level, where Jack's mother had been housekeeper, and where Jack had worked as a stable boy.

'What ho?' said the groom, as Jack and Silver and Crispis clattered into the courtyard, with Sir Boris riding behind. 'What have you brought here, boy?'

'I shall answer no one but the Master of the House,' said Jack, with such authority that the groom summoned the keeper of the yard, and the keeper summoned the livery page, and the page the steward, and after a deal of to-ing and fro-ing, the Master of the House came down the stairs himself, took one look at the Knight and the cart, and the stone boys and Jack's stone mother, and announced that a conversation would take place over beef and pudding, for he had been out and not yet dined.

And Silver said nothing – nothing at all, because as soon as she set eyes on him, she knew just whose house it was, and she began to have a better idea of how she had come here, and why.

The three of them were eating beef and pudding. Silver was

starving hungry, and too busy eating to talk, but she was very keen to listen.

She was looking under her cap at Sir Roger Rover, a fine man with green eyes and a trim red beard. His nose was exactly like Silver's.

'And you say,' said Sir Roger Rover to Jack, 'that this fellow the Magus, previously living in Dark House Lane, wants to turn all of the city of London into gold?'

'He is an alchemist,' said Jack. 'It is his life's work to change one substance into another, and already he can change flesh to stone.'

'I am sorry about your mother,' said Roger Rover. 'She was a very good housekeeper –' then he saw Jack's sad face, 'and, er, a very fine mother, I am sure.'

Jack's mother stood like a statue in the corner of the room. The stone boys had been lined up in the hall. Crispis had gone to be washed, to see if the yellow would come off. Sir Boris was seeing to his horse in the best stable. That was his wish. He did not eat.

'And when will this marvel take place? This marvel of all the dross of the town into solid gold?' asked Sir Roger, who was thinking that a certain amount of gold could do no harm.

'The work began two days ago – I think it was two days ago,' said Jack, 'at the time of the new moon, so there are perhaps twelve days left to the full moon, which I think will eclipse the sun.'

'Indeed, indeed,' said Sir Roger. 'There is such an eclipse, John Dee himself has told me so – he is the Queen's own alchemist and mathematician.'

'I know him,' said Jack, 'for he was my mother's master before she came to you.'

'Indeed, indeed!' said Roger Rover, stroking his beard. 'I had forgotten that. But Jack, the moon is not far from full now – tomorrow, I do believe.'

Jack rubbed his head. 'Then I have been caught in some magic of time at the Dark House – the new moon came, I lent the Magus my power . . . I went to sleep . . .'

And Silver remembered how she had been reading the Book of the Phoenix and had had the strange sensation that time was passing oddly . . .

'He has done it so that he can win!' shouted Jack, getting up from the table. 'We must find him!'

Roger Rover took the boy firmly by the shoulders and settled him back on the bench.

'This frenzy is not the way, Jack. This very night John Dee's own assistant comes to see me on another matter. I shall discuss the whole business with him, and we shall speak of it in the morning. I would not believe a word of it if it were not for the statue of your poor mother, yet . . .'

And Sir Roger Rover went to look at her, sighing and shaking his head.

'Take your mother's rooms as your own, and stay there with this companion of yours – a familiar face, I think?'

And Silver did seem like a familiar face to Sir Roger, but she knew why, and he did not. She smiled and bowed, and said nothing. Sir Roger stood staring at her as she left the room with Jack.

Jack and Silver went upstairs to Jack's mother's tiny sitting room with its small bed in an alcove in the wall. Jack was gloomy that they had lost so much time.

'Jack,' said Silver, 'it may be that he put us both into a swoon of time in the Dark House – it was his house and under his magic, but we are not under his magic now, and we can change what lies ahead.'

'No one can change what lies ahead,' said Jack, his heart heavy.

'That is not true, Jack,' said Silver. 'Nothing is solid, nothing is fixed,' and she said this with such certainty that Jack felt calm again. He smiled.

'I am used to sleeping in the hayloft above the stables,' said Jack. 'I shall sleep on the floor here, and you shall have this bed, Mistress Silver.'

'Call me Silver,' said Silver, 'and remember I am a boy.'

'Yes,' said Jack. 'I shall try.'

'Jack,' said Silver, 'Sir Roger Rover, your master, he's a pirate, isn't he? And a spy?'

Jack looked angry, and now that he had a power about him, he was frightening when he looked angry.

'My master is a sea-faring gentleman close to the Queen herself!' said Jack hotly. 'He has amassed a great fortune through treasure trove, and been granted lands and titles by the Queen. He possesses this fine house in London, one of the very finest, and he has a great estate in Cheshire, with a splendid new-built house.'

'I know that,' said Silver, 'I live there. It's called Tanglewreck.'

Jack looked at her in surprise. 'It is certainly called Tanglewreck,' he said. 'But how can you live there?'

'It's been in our family since Roger Rover built it,' answered Silver. 'The house is falling apart a bit, well, quite a lot now, and we haven't got any of the farms and lands with it at all, they were all sold years and years ago, but the house is still there, and it's mine – well, my parents', but I don't think they're coming back. It's a long story, Jack, but it must be why I am here. It's all tangled together – like the Tanglewreck house. Roger Rover is my ancestor, but I don't think we should tell him. He won't believe me.'

'I don't believe you,' said Jack.

'You've got a cheek,' said Silver. 'Dragons, Eyebats, alchemists, stone boys, bright yellow children, mad old women who live under trees, a knight called Sir Boris, a sunflower that rescued you, creatures cut in half – and me, arriving through the fireplace – and you think it's too hard to believe that Roger Rover is my ancestor and that I live in his house more than four hundred years later? That's the easy bit!'

Jack was silent.

'Right then,' said Silver, 'and I'll tell you something else. It's your task to stop the Magus turning everything into gold, but I'm here to help you, because you called me. But now that I know about Roger Rover, I think I might be here for some other reason too.'

'What could that be?' asked Jack.

'It's to do with an adventure I had before you met me. You call me the Golden Maiden, and yes, Jack, I am her, though in other places I'm known as the Girl with the Golden Face.'

'What other places?' said Jack.

'I'll tell you the whole story as we go along,' said Silver, 'but, Jack, Roger Rover says he has a visitor tonight – and I'd like to see who it is . . . is there a way that we can watch out?'

THE VISITOR

At seven o'clock precisely, the Visitor entered the inner chamber of Sir Roger Rover.

The Visitor was never late, unless he meant to be, and never early, unless he intended it. He used time as though he owned it, which, one day, he hoped to do.

But that day was not today and that night was not tonight. Tonight he was coming to buy a clock, or the pieces of one.

Jack and Silver were squashed together behind a secret panel that Jack's mother had shown him. The panel opened into the inner chamber, with holes in that looked like air vents, but were really spy holes to see through.

The two of them had a very good view of the room; its fireplace, its carved wooden table and chair, its cabinet, its bookcase. Roger Rover was in the room already, looking out of the window and on to the river. There was a brief knock at the door, and the Visitor entered.

'Sir Roger!' said a voice, and Silver nearly shouted out, because she knew the voice, and she knew the figure of the man, though he was young here, and not nearly as fat as . . . the . . . man . . .

'Abel Darkwater,' announced Roger Rover, pouring wine from a silver jug.

. . . she . . . had . . . met . . . so fatefully . . . at . . . Tanglewreck . . . two years ago (or four hundred and twelve years later, depending on how you thought about time); the man who had imprisoned her first in his house, and finally in a giant glass alembic like the ones Jack had worked in the Dark House.

Abel Darkwater was a small man with short legs but a powerfully built upper body. His chest was wide and that made his arms seem too short. His hands were thick and heavy, with dark hair on the backs and finger joints, and his eyes, protruding a little, were very round, like two orbs. He had a quiet voice, but there was an edge of threat to it, so that even when he was saying good morning it sounded as though it might not be a good morning for you if he had anything to do with it.

The last time Silver had seen him he had been fatter and balder and older, though his voice was just the same. Now, he still had a coating of dark hair on his head, worn close like a skull cap, and coarse and bristly. And he had long whiskers. *A boar!* thought Silver. *He looks like a man who is really a boar.*

Abel Darkwater took the wine and drank it down.

'My master John Dee has asked me to bring you this gold in return for a clock,' said Abel Darkwater, plonking down a very large velvet bag on the table.

'I do not need gold,' said Roger Rover, 'and I hear, from the gossip in the streets, that the whole city will very soon be made of gold. Tell me straightforwardly, Darkwater, do you have any information about a man who calls himself the

232

Magus? An alchemist? Recently to be found in Dark House Lane?'

'There was such a man,' replied Abel Darkwater, 'and we knew of him, oh, yes, but this night he takes a boat across the Channel to France.'

'Not turning London into solid gold, then?' asked Sir Roger, refilling the goblets with dark red wine.

'A fantasy, an idle dream,' said Abel Darkwater. 'Only the true alchemist can turn lead into gold. The Magus, as he calls himself, is a fool and an impostor – he has been found out, and that is why he is fleeing these shores. My master John Dee has nothing to do with him.'

'I am glad to hear it,' said Roger Rover, 'but tell me, why does your master John Dee want the pieces of this clock? It is broken, and has no value but for its jewels, which are beautiful but not exceptional.'

'May I see it?' asked Abel Darkwater, his breath a little short.

Roger Rover unlocked his cabinet, and drew out a battered leather bag, sea-stained and cracked. Then he spread his handkerchief on his desk and emptied on to it the contents of the bag.

What a mess! Springs, cogs, enamelled pictures, rubies, pearls, bits of gold . . .

Silver thought she would have a heart attack. There it was, the Timekeeper. The clock that could control time. The clock that even now, no, not now, four hundred years later, where she lived, was ticking at Tanglewreck. She had a sudden fearful thought: was it really Jack who had called her to help him, or had some sinister power set out to trap her?

Abel Darkwater ran his hands over the pieces. 'It is a clock,' he murmured, 'unlike any other clock. It has a mysterious power, useless to you, but of great interest to my master. Let me buy it. Let me take it.'

Roger Rover suddenly swept up the pieces and put them back into the leather bag. 'It is not for sale,' he said firmly.

'It is better,' said Abel Darkwater quietly, but with that threat in his voice, 'that you be a friend to us, Roger Rover, and not an enemy. My master is a powerful man, alchemist to the Queen herself, oh, yes, a powerful man, and not a man, I should hazard, that you wish to offend.'

'I offend no man,' said Roger Rover mildly, 'yet perhaps your master should visit me himself, if this clock means such a great deal to him. I do not say he cannot have it – I say it is not for sale. There may be another price that suits us both – but you are the servant, and I must deal with the master. Send John Dee to me, or bid that I shall come to him.'

Silver could see how angry was Abel Darkwater, so angry that he levitated slightly above the floor. How well she remembered him doing that! Roger Rover appeared not to notice. Bowing his head slightly and curtly, Abel Darkwater left the room.

'We have to follow him!' whispered Silver to Jack. Jack wanted to ask why, but the look on Silver's face was so serious and urgent that, without speaking, Jack led Silver through a maze of dusty passages and out on to the river, just as Abel

234

Darkwater was getting into his rowboat.

'Run upriver with me,' said Jack, 'if you want to keep him in sight!'

'I'll explain it all!' said Silver. 'I promise!'

Abel Darkwater rowed on until he came to an inn at the waterside. It was a strange inn, thought Silver, called Le Swan on Le Hope, and its sign was a golden swan holding a maiden in its beak.

'Pull your cap down,' said Jack. 'There will be danger.'

Jack and Silver slunk inside the inn. It was a low-roofed, timber-framed place with sawdust all over the floor, and heavy oak barrels that served as places to sit or places to eat. There were squat benches too, crammed five men to a bench, and children playing a dice game by the window.

Jack bought himself and Silver some pudding and small beer, a kind of watery beer that children drank, and that Silver had read about but never tasted; it was horrible.

Abel Darkwater had ordered Spanish wine and he sat at a table in the window.

'Jack,' said Silver, 'I know you called me to help you, but I'm scared, because that man Abel Darkwater is very power-ful, and he lives on, through time. He's still alive in my world, four hundred and more years away, and all he wants is to control time – and to do that he needs that clock that you saw, the Timekeeper, and he needs me. Well, no, he doesn't need me, he needs me not to exist.'

'Dead?' said Jack.

'More or less,' said Silver. 'If I get lost and locked in time here, then in the future, I won't be able to defeat him. But –'

'No,' said Jack, 'and I brought you here. I called you.'

'I know,' said Silver, 'but . . .'

But at that moment, who should come through the door to join Abel Darkwater, but the Magus himself?

By now the tavern was full of evening drinkers, and working men taking their supper of pigs' trotters and eels and cabbage soup and thick black bread, and suet pudding stuffed with sheep's brains.

'Did you just say sheeps' brains?' said Silver, who had been eating her pudding quite happily until then.

'Silver, I cannot go nearer to the Magus, he will know me,' said Jack, 'but your disguise is good. Can you not tag on to those apprentice boys and get by his table, and see what you can find?'

Silver didn't like the thought of going nearer to either the Magus or Abel Darkwater, but it was true that she no longer looked like herself, whereas Jack looked just like himself.

She pulled her cap lower and slipped off her stool.

The apprentice boys piling into the tavern were rowdy and lively, and hardly noticed Silver crewing along with them as they shoved themselves and their brimming pots of ale into the space by the fire. Silver stood with her back so close to Abel Darkwater that she could feel the warmth of him through his cloak.

The Magus was talking.

'The Opus has begun. It will be completed at the eclipse and the rise of the tides. If you will assist me I shall make you a wealthy man, Darkwater. You shall leave John Dee and be your own master.'

'I am my own master,' replied Darkwater, 'for I owe nothing to John Dee. I have left his service, and have a work of my own to accomplish. You seek gold, but I seek the gold that cannot be counted.'

'I will not interfere with your own work,' said the Magus. 'That is yours. Yet I need an assistant. What is your price?'

'Riches,' said Abel Darkwater, 'enough that I may flee to France and live without thought of money. There is a clock I must obtain, and when I have obtained it, I must repair it. A great deal of money will be necessary.'

'The Timekeeper?' laughed the Magus. 'You are a fool, Darkwater, if you believe that timepiece has any power. It is a toy, the story is a rumour. There is nothing there.'

'Then let my folly be my own,' replied Darkwater evenly. 'And my price is something more than gold . . .'

The Magus looked at him steadily.

'I want the Captive.'

'She is disappeared,' said the Magus.

'But she is with the boy, of that I am sure. He called her.'

'How do you know that?' said the Magus sharply.

'She is the Golden Maiden,' said Abel Darkwater.

'That cannot be!' said the Magus.

'Perhaps you do not know all that you think you know.

Perhaps you do not control all that you think you control,' said Abel Darkwater quietly.

The Magus was silent. He was so angry that a part of the table began to smoulder. Abel Darkwater put his hand over the smoking smouldering wood, and the smoke rose up between his thick fingers. He was smiling. It was unpleasant.

'The boy is your rival, do not underestimate him. Be aware too that the Maiden has power of her own.'

'I shall destroy the boy,' said the Magus. 'As to this Maiden . . .'

'If you want my help, do not bargain with me. When you take the boy, give me the girl. The money is the money, but the girl is the price. No more and no less.'

The Magus nodded. 'You shall have the money, and you shall have the Maiden.'

'I shall join you in the morning, before dawn,' said Abel Darkwater. 'I have things to do until then. Where shall I find you?'

'At the old Priory,' said the Magus, and Abel Darkwater laughed his short unpleasant laugh.

'And the Abbess? Will she be there too?'

'She has some interest in the Work,' said the Magus. 'The old Priory, then . . .'

The Magus rose. Silver took the opportunity to slip away under cover of an oaf the size of an elephant. This oaf, carrying six empty flagons of ale to be replenished, was so fat and vast that neither the Magus nor Abel Darkwater noticed Silver at all. In a flash she was back to where she had left Jack, sitting on a barrel. But Jack had gone outside, and was crouching behind a mooring stone, listening to Wedge and Mistress Split, waiting at oars in the sullen golden boat.

'Thing won't hatch!' said Wedge. 'If I could hatch it, I could take all his power, all his money, all his golden city, but the thing won't hatch. Had every hen in London sit on it, but hatch it will not.'

'I don't care one tittle!' snarled Mistress Split. 'What wouldn't I give of gold and jewels to see my beautiful Boojie again. Mine mine mine! Gone gone gone!'

'Shut up!' shouted Wedge. 'I hated that dog, all four legs and fur and two eyes and whole. We doesn't do wholes, we does halves, as well you know!'

'Mine mine mine,' moaned Mistress Split, 'and the Magus forcing us to work all day and all night, and all hollow it is to me now, even when this city is paved with gold and we gets a golden house with a golden front door.'

'There will be no golden house or golden front door,' said Wedge. 'He'll shove us back in a bottle and drown us. If you won't help me with the hatching of the Egg, and join me in halves by rights, then I'll save myself and let you drown.'

'Give me the Egg!' cried Mistress Split. 'I'll take it to Mother Midnight – she won't speak to you, as she speaks only to women and children and never to men.'

'She's a stupid old woman,' said Wedge.

'She has power,' said Mistress Split, 'and well may she have the hen that can hatch the Egg.'

And privately Mistress Split was thinking that if she could only get away from Wedge for an hour, she could find her beloved Boojie dog.

Jack heard – and thought that if he needed to find the Magus, all he had to do was follow Mistress Split when she left Mother Midnight.

Then he shrank back, for the Magus himself was coming towards the boat.

MORE VISITORS

At the house on the Strand called The Level, Roger Rover was perplexed. No sooner had Abel Darkwater left the house by the water-gate, than with a great clattering and racket, a coach had pulled into the outer courtyard, and a distinguished gentleman had come flying through the inner courtyard, holding on to his hat as he ran, and demanding to see Sir Roger. It was John Dee himself, alchemist to Queen Elizabeth.

'Darkwater!' panted Dee. 'He has been here, I know! Did he get it?'

'If you are referring to the pieces of the clock, no, he did not. Indeed I bid him ask you to attend on me yourself over this matter, though I confess I did not expect you so soon.'

'It was not I who sent him!' said John Dee. 'He is no longer my apprentice – I turned him out a month ago when I discovered his true motives and meddlings. He has put himself in the service of the dark powers.'

'And the Magus?' asked Roger Rover.

'The man who calls himself the Magus is an impostor. He is no true alchemist. My spies tell me he is about to leave for France.'

'Then mayhap he has taken Darkwater with him – there

was some talk, some gossip, some rumour, of the city of London turned to gold.'

'That cannot happen,' said John Dee flatly. 'Impossible. Gossip. Superstitious talk of foolish folk of the kind the Magus so easily deceived. That man is nothing to our purpose or interest, I do assure you. Yet, I believe it would be wise for you to entrust that timepiece to me.'

'Why should I?' said Roger Rover.

'So that it is not stolen from you! It has a power, I admit, or it may have a power – I do not know. It has a history, and I must study it.'

'It is not for sale,' said Roger Rover. 'I got it in Rome, you know. Very recently.'

John Dee laughed and sat down, fanning himself with his hat. 'You were spying for the Queen, as well I know, and I know that this clock was given to you as a bribe!'

'It seems that the Queen has spies to spy on her spies . . .' said Roger Rover drily.

'But of course,' said John Dee. 'She cannot be too careful . . .' John Dee paused. 'I know well,' he said, 'that the clock is in pieces because the Pope himself smashed it to the floor in front of the sorceress who tried to trade it for her life. You were in the room at the time.'

'Yes, she was a woman of considerable authority – no doubt now burned to death.'

'For witchcraft no doubt,' said John Dee, 'and yet I would like to see the pieces of the clock – may I?'

There was a pause, a long pause. Roger Rover took out

the sea-stained bag once more, and John Dee examined the pieces, and in particular the strange pictures that decorated the twin faces of the clock.

'The Timekeeper . . .' said John Dee, more to himself than Roger Rover. 'If it had the power that is claimed for it – then any man would prefer it to a thousand cities made of gold . . .'

'But it is just a broken clock,' said Roger Rover, returning the parts to the bag, 'and it is my broken clock . . .'

John Dee left the house, Roger Rover taking him through the hall himself, carrying a candlestick. As he made his way back, he stopped to look at the statue of Jack's mother. As he looked, he saw something very strange and very unlikely begin to happen before his eyes. The bleak stone chisels of her hair were turning to gold.

THE BOOK OF THE PHOENIX

Down at the river by Le Swan on Le Hope, Silver and Jack were arguing.

'The old Priory, Jack, and the Magus and Abel Darkwater are in it together for certain, but we've got until tomorrow. If we go back to Sir Roger Rover's, we can look at the Book of the Phoenix. There may be clues.'

But Jack wanted to go straight after the Magus.

'Jack,' said Silver, 'there is more to this than the City of Gold. There is a story of mine underneath this story of yours.'

'The clock?' asked Jack, and Silver nodded.

'Yes, the Timekeeper.'

'But,' said Jack, 'if all that be true and so, your story is four hundred years away, and mine is now, and will be finished tomorrow, unless I defeat the Magus.'

'Our stories are together. Yours is mine and mine is yours. But we need to read the Book, Jack. I know there's something in there that will help us both. I can't do it without you, though, because it is written in Latin.'

'I know but a little Latin,' said Jack, hesitating.

'Well, I know none,' said Silver.

'That is because girls do not go to school,' said Jack.

'We do in the future,' said Silver, 'but we don't do Latin any more.'

Jack looked at Silver and smiled his gentle shy smile. 'I don't want you to be killed,' he said. 'Let's go back and find the Book.'

The house on the Strand was quiet and dark as the two of them crept back in. The Book was upstairs in Jack's mother's little room, and Silver used the tinderbox to light a small fire and to flare the candles. She got down the Book and began turning the pages.

Jack was deep in thought, and moving sadly amongst his mother's things – her brush and comb, her spare dress, her ink pen, her little easel and oils where she liked to paint pictures. He wondered what it was like to be made of stone, and if she knew she was made of stone, and if her living soul was sitting inside her stone body, or if she knew nothing at all, no more than does a stone.

At least Sir Boris was guarding her from further harm, and if he, Jack, could only defeat the Magus, he knew he could set his mother free . . .

Sighing, he took the Dragon's sunflower seeds out of his pocket – there were three left – and put them carefully in a little silver egg cup of his mother's, on top of the mantelpiece.

'I'm sure we will need them for something soon,' he said to Silver, 'and I don't want them to be lost or stolen.'

Silver nodded absently; she was trying to read the Book.

The house was very still. Then . . .

'There's someone outside,' said Jack. 'Listen!'

Sure enough, from behind the door, on the corridor, came footsteps, light and pattering, but footsteps nonetheless. The footsteps stopped outside the door.

'Spy through the keyhole,' whispered Silver.

Jack bent down and put his eye to the keyhole. He jumped back in horror – there was a gleaming eye on the other side.

'Who goes there?' said Jack. 'Who goes there, I say?'

'Me,' piped a tiny voice.

Jack opened the door. There was Crispis, and beside him was Max the dog. The dog was the dog, as doggy as you would expect, and black and gleaming, and looking like a fine dog should, but Crispis was still bright yellow, his arms, his legs, his clothes, his body, his curly hair; but his face was coal-black, as quite coal-black as Max's. He looked exactly like a sunflower.

'It wouldn't wash off,' he said, by way of explanation, 'and then this afternoon, my face turned black like my hair! I wish I was in a garden, growing, and not here at all.'

The little child went and sat by the fire, sunk in his own thoughts.

'Is he all right?' asked Silver.

'He's Crispis,' said Jack. 'That's how he is, even when he isn't yellow and black.'

Silver and Jack turned back to the Book of the Phoenix.

In hoc lapide sunt quatuor elementa et assimulatur mundo et mundi compositioni . . .

'What's this all about?' asked Silver. Jack was puzzling over the words – *four elements, the lapis* . . . He read on, *the red lily and the white lily, elixir of honey, dog's mercury, sea-dew, the wine of Tartarus* . . .

'Keep going,' said Silver. 'Where's that drawing of you?'

Jack found the page of the Radiant Boy. There was a long text beneath. 'I can't read this,' he said. 'It's very hard Latin.'

'Give it to me,' said Crispis. 'I learned Latin as soon as I was born, to serve the Magus.'

The leather-bound book was so heavy that Crispis couldn't hold it, so Jack stood him on a stool with the book on a table so that he could read the paragraphs.

'The Adept will take the power freely given from the Radiant Boy and join that power to his own to complete the Work. Only when the planets are aligned as described, and only when the moon covers the sun, and only when the power is given, and only when the tidal waters rise, can the substance that is not gold become gold. And before this the Adept will have made all manner of preparations as described. And he who seeks the dark power must make a sacrifice, and that sacrifice must be blood most dear.'

Crispis stopped reading. 'Horrible,' he said. 'Blood most dear!'

Jack stood up. 'Silver, if there is an eclipse of the sun by the moon tomorrow, and the Thames rises, then the Magus will turn the city to gold.'

'How can we find out about the tides?' asked Silver.

'We will ask the Keeper of the Tides,' said Jack. 'We must go to London Bridge.'

'Wait,' said Silver, and she turned the pages of the Book once more, and there she was, looking like herself, and underneath, in Latin, was written *The Golden Maiden*, and in her hands, the Timekeeper.

'*She is Time*,' said Crispis. 'It says no more.'

'What have I to do with the Radiant Boy?' she said. 'We are holding hands.'

'He is your Brother in Time,' said Crispis.

'Look,' said Crispis, and there on another page was the Dragon, and there was the Knight Summoned.

'What does this mean, Crispis?' asked Silver, and the child read faithfully. '*There is a battle*,' he said, '*a battle for the sun*. No, that's not right, it says, *The Battle of the Sun*.'

'Who wins it?' asked Silver, but Crispis shook his head. 'That is where the Book ends.'

And the rest of the pages were blank and empty.

'We must go right away to London Bridge!' cried Jack, agitated.

'Jack,' said Silver, 'it's the middle of the night. I think we should try and sleep until just before dawn. We might be awake for days and days after this.'

'I'd like to go to sleep,' said Crispis, curling up on a cushion like a cat; a yellow and black cat.

Jack looked uneasy, but then Max already had his nose in his paws by the fire, and Silver was preparing blankets. Jack realised he was very tired indeed, and soon all of them were breathing deeply in the dark and quiet of the chamber, by the low-glowing fire.

Jack was dreaming.

He dreamed he was in a cave and that two bright uncanny eyes were staring at him, just an inch from his face. Without moving, he opened his own eyes, and let out a terrible scream; two bright uncanny eyes were so close to his own that they were like his own eyes in a mirror.

At his scream, the Eyebat flew to the curtain rail and hung there. Silver, Crispis and Max woke up all together to find Jack on his feet with his mother's hairnet in his hands.

'Catch it!' he commanded. 'This is our chance!'

And for the next ten minutes the room was in uproar as children and dogs and Eyebats chased each other round and round so that it was hard to say how many there were of each.

Silver had the fire bellows, and she used pumps of air to drive the Eyebat off any perch, while Max refused to let it touch the ground and shuffle behind a cupboard. Crispis stood on a stool in the middle of the room like a ringmaster, shouting, 'Horrible Eyebat,' and perhaps it was this unflattering description, or perhaps the jets of dusty air, or the dog's long jaws, or something determined about Jack, but suddenly the Eyebat stopped its flapping, and fell uselessly into the hairnet.

'Box!' shouted Jack. 'Sewing box!'

Silver grabbed Jack's mother's sewing box, opened the lid,

took out the top tray of needles and pins, and Jack slammed the netted Eyebat in among the coloured threads, and shut and locked the lid.

'One less thing to worry about,' he said. 'Now, we must begin the day – all of you, let us go.'

But while Jack and Silver were making ready, Crispis, not really knowing why he did it, stole one of the remaining three sunflower seeds that the Dragon had given to Jack, and, opening the lid of the sewing box, fed it to the Eyebat.

'Horrible Eyebat,' he said to himself, 'but even so, you should not be starved to death.'

Jack did not notice. The two remaining seeds were on the mantelpiece where he had left them.

And the three of them left the house on the Strand called The Level, and set off, Max trotting beside them, into the just-whitening day towards London Bridge.

THE KEEPER OF
THE TIDES

On London Bridge, hanging over the river like a wasp's nest hangs from a branch over a stream, hung the perilous, precarious poop-house of the Keeper of the Tides.

This house had one room, and looked in every respect like the stern of a galleon, where the captain would have his wide windows, and his dinner table and decanter, and where he could observe the vast sea that bore his vessel.

In truth, the Keeper of the Tides favoured the dress of a sea captain, and wore naval breeches and stockings, both very dirty, and a studded leather coat. His hair, which was thick and white, was brushed back very neat, and tied in a pigtail.

The poop-house was crammed every inch with maps rolled up and fastened with red ribbon, with almanacs of the moon and the tides, with rain gauges and weather gauges, and windsocks to determine the direction of the wind, and plumb lines, to measure the rising river, and nets for hauling things out, and a rope ladder slung out of the window dropping straight into the official tidal barge.

In the barge, the Keeper inspected the condition of the wharves and jetties, and of the silt pans and eel stocks, the ebb and flow, the rise and fall – indeed, everything to do with a river that needed doing and that could be done.

The Keeper slept in a hammock slung from side to side of his poop, and he cooked on a brazier fuelled with driftwood that his boy collected at low tide.

When Jack and Silver arrived, with Crispis and Max keeping up the rear, the Keeper was sitting in his window with two lighted candles, and a telescope, consulting the last passage of the dawn stars.

He seemed pleased to see Jack, for he remembered that his mother had been searching for him.

'Pray say what is that strange element you have with you?' asked the Keeper, looking at Crispis, who did look quite odd with his coal-black face and yellow body.

'He has been eating sunflower seeds,' said Jack, which was hardly an explanation, unless you knew what kind of sunflower seeds.

But the Keeper just nodded. 'Most dangerous. Seeds are quite untrustworthy, for they contain in themselves their whole nature, and might, as in this case here, root and grow, and quite occupy the person. Better to eat fish.'

Then the Keeper looked at Silver, dressed as a boy, her cap pulled low.

'This is my friend, Silver, and my dog Max,' said Jack.

'And does your mother know that you are out so early?' asked the Keeper.

'My mother is in difficulties,' said Jack. 'As am I. We need your advice on the tides, and then we shall return to Mother Midnight, and see what help or divination she can offer us.'

The Keeper shook his head. 'Mother Midnight has vanished. As of yesterday night. I went there myself for my rheumatism – she gives me an ointment of myrtle and dog grease in return for fish for herself and her cat. I am one of the few members of the grown male race who can speak to her and be answered. For as you know, she is a witch, and one of those witches who do not consort with men. Surely she is a lady of strange ways but undeniable powers. I was quite put out to find her gone, yes, gone. I cannot understand it, as she has lived there for at least one hundred years.'

Jack and Silver exchanged glances. 'Did you see any other person?' asked Jack.

'But one,' replied the Keeper. 'Extraordinary, a thing, a female, who seemed as if she had been cut in half, straight down the middle, as you would split and serve a salmon.'

'Did you speak with this woman?' asked Jack.

'I did not. She was hurrying to a boat where a second creature, almost as bizarre, was calling to her in a rough fashion. There was a large crate in the boat. It was not a craft I recognise, and I recognise most. It was a dull golden colour, quite distinctive.'

Crispis was gazing out of the poop-window. 'That boat . . .' he said, in his usual elliptical way.

Jack and Silver and the Keeper went to the window. Sure enough, passing beneath the bridge were Wedge and Mistress Split. The Keeper opened the window.

'YOU THERE!' he shouted.

'YAH!' yelled Wedge. 'YAH HAH HAH!' and rowed on.

But at that moment, Max put his paws up at the window and let out three short sharp barks. Mistress Split spun round her head as though it were on a swivel, and saw the dog.

'BOOJIE! BOOJIE! BOOJIE!' she cried, and she dropped her one oar into the water, and stood up on her one leg, waving her one arm as though she had found her heart's desire.

Which she had.

Max was not so sure, and jumped down and hid under the table.

Then, as Wedge was trying to pull her back down, and she was shrieking like a fishwife about the pain of love and loss, the boat keeled to the left, then it keeled to the right, then half the river slopped into it one side and slopped out the other side, and Wedge was waving his oar like a drowning man, which was perhaps a good thing, as the boat suddenly tipped over and the two of them were in the river.

'Bless my best breeches!' said the Keeper of the Tides.

'Now what?' asked Silver, whose previous adventures and strange life meant that very little perturbed her.

'I am bound by the high calling of my Office to SAVE THEM,' cried the Keeper. 'They are Thames mariners.'

'I don't think so,' said Crispis, heartily hoping they would both drown.

'Jack! Help me lower the net, come on, come on!'

And Jack, because he was the gentlest, kindest boy on earth, as well as one of the most powerful, though he did not know it, began to lower the net.

But Wedge was not a man to be rescued. He kicked and reached, and reached and kicked, and made his half-mad way to the half-sunk boat, and by diving underneath, and pushing like a porpoise, he managed to right it. Then he was off, rowing with one arm and one oar in crazy circles downriver, and luckily for him the tide was on his side, and away he went, darkening, darkening now into the gloom of the river.

But Mistress Split was floundering.

'To the net! To the net!' cried the Keeper. 'Swim to the net, good lady!'

And at last, with a spluttering and a spitting and a flailing and a sinking and a soaking, head under, head up, one minute drowned and one minute saved, Mistress Split flopped into the net like a mors marina, the death-fish feared by sailors the world over. There she was, on her back, coughing up her one lung.

'Haul! Haul!' cried the Keeper, and had it not been for Jack's great strength, far surpassing the strength of ten men, Mistress Split would have met her fate at the bottom of the river. As it was, she found herself beached and broken like an old boat, lying on the deck of the poop.

'Now, mistress, now now!' fussed the Keeper, and gave her rum.

Yet she lay there, her eye glassy.

Like a saint, Max slunk out from under the table, and if ever a dog had a halo over his ears, it was this dog. He licked the cold and river-soaked face of the Creature.

'Boojie!' she whispered, and spewed up two pints of river

water, containing a grey pearl and a small herring.

Hot rum followed by burnt toast seemed to revive her. And she sat in her own puddle on the floor, alternately cooing over Max, and expostulating on the bitterness of fate, that half drowns a woman before she can be reunited with her love.

The Keeper of the Tides drew Jack to one side.

'My boy,' he said, 'you seem to know this, this, er, lady. Tell me true, is she, er, cut in two?'

'She is,' answered Jack, 'and the other one on the boat, Wedge, he is her other half. They were made in the same bottle.'

'You mean that she is not a Freak of Nature?'

'No, for she was made and not born.'

'And who was it, that by some black art, accomplished this task?'

'His name is the Magus. An alchemist. Formerly of Dark House Lane. I am seeking him. It is his strong desire and purpose to turn the whole city of London into solid gold.'

'Gold!' exclaimed the Keeper of the Tides. 'Why, my boy, look at this!' And he pulled out the small golden fish that he had fished out of the Thames.

'What day was this?' asked Jack.

'August the fourteenth!' replied the Keeper, and Jack realised it had been the day of his birthday and the day of his kidnapping.

'It was the day that I became the Radiant Boy,' he said

softly, more to himself than to anyone else.

The Keeper of the Tides looked grave. 'Is this Magus of whom you speak a short gentleman, powerfully built and bristled, something of a boar about him, yes, a boar, and with round eyes like two orbs?'

'No,' said Silver, who had overheard, 'that's another one of them. Another alchemist, I mean. I mean, you have quite a lot of them in Elizabethan times, on account of not having any science yet – chemistry in particular . . .'

The Keeper of the Tides looked blank. 'Chemistry?'

'Yeah, you've got alchemistry, and later, you just get chemistry – when the magic's gone.'

'I don't want the magic to go,' said Crispis.

'Well, it hasn't done you much good, has it?' said Silver. 'You've eaten the Dragon's sunflower and turned yellow and black.'

'My sunflower rescued you,' said Crispis, and then he paused, 'but it didn't rescue me,' and then he looked sad.

The Keeper of the Tides held up his hands. 'Tell me the name of the short boar of a man who came to me yesternight seeking report of today's tides.'

'Abel Darkwater,' said Silver.

'Are you acquainted with him?' asked the Keeper of the Tides.

'He once shut me in a giant alembic and tried to boil me alive, and before that, I had to escape from his house, so yes, I suppose I am acquainted with him,' said Silver.

'You did not tell me that part of the story,' said Jack,

'about the boiling!'

'I didn't want to worry you,' said Silver.

'But if you know where he lives . . .'

'He doesn't live there yet,' said Silver. 'His house, the one I went to, isn't built until 1720, and it is only 1601 at present.'

The Keeper of the Tides was baffled. Before anyone could try and explain, Mistress Split gave another great cough and lurched up a piece of lead piping.

'I can hear all that you tell,' she said, 'and I can tell you something, as you have rescued me. The Magus and Abel Darkwater are to meet this very dawn by the old Priory outside of the city wall, down Hog Lane, through the Bishops Gate. There is a piece of land called the Spital Field . . .'

'That's funny,' said Silver.

'No call for amusement or to interrupt me!' said Mistress Split crossly.

'I mean funny queer, not funny ha-ha,' said Silver. 'It's just that, where Abel Darkwater will live, when he lives there, when his house is built, is in Spitalfields – that's where I stayed. Spital is an old word for hospital, isn't it?'

'There used to be a hospital in the old Priory of St Mary – known to all as St Mary Spital,' said Jack, 'but that was years ago, and now the Priory is abandoned and the chapel ruined – the Abbess fled to France.'

'Bless me, you seem to know much about the old religion, Jack,' said the Keeper of the Tides mildly.

'My family has some sympathy with the old religion,' said Jack, looking worried, for in the reign of Elizabeth, only traitors were Catholics now, and the penalty was death.

'Roger Rover is Catholic,' said Silver, 'my family has always been Catholic.'

'Silver! Be quiet!' said Jack.

But the Keeper of the Tides shook his head, smiling, 'There are many who must hide their faith,' he said. 'Your mother is my friend, Jack, and you have nothing to fear, and neither, I am sure does, a gentleman, a favourite of the Queen, such as be Sir Roger Rover.'

Jack relaxed. Silver was sorry for blurting things out, and took his hand.

'All the waste and filth of London finds its way east!' said Mistress Split doomfully. 'The old Priory is a place for dark magic, as is well known – and the Abbess whom you claim to be in France, well I claim otherwise!'

Before Mistress Split could be questioned on these remarks, the Keeper of the Tides jumped up from where he had been chalking calculations on a piece of slate, and consulting his tables.

'This is the matter of the tides! The eclipse of the sun by the moon is very strange and the nearness of the moon to the Earth will indeed cause the Thames to rise, this very day. I did not check the figures when I spoke to the man called Darkwater, but now I see that it will be a very considerable rising.'

'Then that will allow the Magus to complete his work,'

said Jack. 'The planets will align, as he foretold, and the waters will rise, just as it says in the Book of the Phoenix, and he will succeed in turning the city into gold!'

'What are we to do?' cried the Keeper. 'How are we to prevent this dreadful event?'

'Never stop the Magus, can't be done!' said Mistress Split, split between gloom and satisfaction.

'Mistress Split,' said Jack. 'What has happened to Mother Midnight? Has the Magus taken her?'

'Wedge, it was,' answered Mistress Split. 'Kidnapping, it was. Making her hatch the Egg, he is.'

'What, hatch it herself?' asked Silver.

'I daresay you are as stupid as Jackster,' said Mistress Split. 'By her arts she can find the creature that can hatch the Egg, and release the magical animal that hides inside, and that animal, what'ere it be, so secret to the Magus, will belong to Wedge.'

'But not to you,' said Jack. 'Wedge has abandoned you. Help us and we will reward you and protect you.'

Mistress Split looked cunning. 'If I take you to where the Magus and Abel Darkwater wait and work, what shall you give me?'

'Riches,' said Jack, not knowing where he would get them from.

Mistress Split shook her head. 'Give me the Boojie dog! Mine own for ever!'

'No,' said Jack. 'He is my dog. I love him.'

'Love?' shouted Mistress Split. 'LOVE? I am the one who

268

loves him, and if love it is that owns the dog, then he is mine mine mine!' and she wrapped the poor dog in her bosom. He only yelped once.

'It is an unhappy bargain, I say it is,' said the Keeper of the Tides, 'yet, you must make it, I fear. You have so little time left!'

Jack was silent. Then he went and knelt by Max and whispered to him, and none could hear what he said, but the dog could hear, and understood, his intelligent head cocked to one side.

Jack stood up. 'Mistress Split, do you swear that you will take us to the place where we should go, without treachery or betrayal, and that it is the true place where I shall find the Magus?'

'I do solemnly swear,' said Mistress Split.

'Then I accept the bargain,' said Jack, and sadly, but firmly, he led Max to his new keeper, who hopped all round the poop-house with delight.

'Now, mistress,' said the Keeper of the Tides, 'wringing wet though you are, a bargain has been made and you must do your part. I give you leave to take my small rowboat, and pray you return it to me when you are able.'

It was an unlikely troupe and a strange sight that left the poop-house on London Bridge and packed themselves into the rowboat beneath. But soon, with Jack pulling strongly on the oars, they were moving rapidly along the Thames to a mooring place as directed by Mistress Split, sitting triumphantly in the prow with the dog on a lead-rope in her lap.

'We have come outside the city walls,' she said, 'and now you must follow me to the old Priory.'

THE PLOT THICKENS

Mistress Split hopped from the boat, and while Jack was mooring it securely, she took out one of the many keys that hung at her belt, and opened a little iron door in a wall. This door led deep underground, and soon Jack and Silver and Crispis and Max were holding on to each other as they followed the hop-hopping sound of Mistress Split and her dim, ill-burning flare.

There were rats everywhere, and horrible dripping noises, and once, Mistress Split held up her flare and gave a dark laugh; there chained to the wall, long left without hope, was a skeleton.

'This passage is secret,' she said, 'and was made by the monks fleeing Good King Henry in the Year of Our Lord 1539.'

'That must have been the dissolution of the monasteries,' said Silver, to herself, pleased that history could sometimes be useful.

'Many were the secrets in the keeping of the Priory, and the Abbess,' said Mistress Split. 'For you should know that the Abbess is an ally of the Magus.'

'I thought she had fled to France,' said Silver.

'They that flee flee for a purpose and they that return

return for a purpose,' said Mistress Split enigmatically.

'She must be very old,' said Silver, 'this Abbess. The Priory has been dissolved for about sixty years . . .'

'She is neither old nor not old,' said Mistress Split, hopping along. 'Old is as time does. But what is time to her? You are as stupid as you seem.'

Silver didn't mind being thought stupid; it meant that her enemies wouldn't be watching out for her to be clever.

'Ho,' called Jack from the rear. 'Ho there!'

Looking round, Silver saw that water was entering the tunnels.

''Tis the rise of the tide,' muttered Mistress Split. 'Out, out,' and, lifting her skirts, she hopped through the water beginning to flow around her foot, and with surprising strength in her single arm, pulled herself up a wormy ladder on the wall, and popped out in a dark alley, close by the Priory of St Mary Spital.

The rest followed her, and stood in a circle like conspirators. 'I had thought to bring you nearer,' she said, 'inside the very walls, but the water has prevented us. Yet . . .' and she pointed at the high wall. 'The Magus will be found in the ruins of the chapel – the old papal chapel. Now you must manage alone, for I have brought you as I said.'

'Where are you going?' asked Jack.

'To find Wedge,' answered Mistress Split. Then she went to Jack, and took the lead-rope from his hand, and turned away. Max looked back once, and whined once, and then he vanished round the corner with Mistress Split.

'Silver,' said Jack, 'take Crispis with you and follow her if you are able. I shall find the Magus.'

'We should stick together,' said Silver, but Jack shook his head.

'The task is mine as you told me, and right it is that it should be so. Today he will be defeated.'

Silver nodded. 'But why do you want me to go after Mistress Split?'

'Mother Midnight will be with Wedge,' said Jack, 'and for my own mother's sake, Mother Midnight must be saved.'

Jack leapt over the ruined Priory wall and was gone.

'Come on, Crispis!' said Silver. 'Let's run after Mistress Split – there she goes, up ahead . . .'

The inner enclosure of the old Priory was still used for growing herbs and small vegetables, and although it was only just dawn, men and boys were already beginning work tending the plants.

Jack pulled his own cap low over his eyes, and stealthily took a wooden wheelbarrow and a fork, and went among the lettuces. He had to find his way to the ruined chapel.

He saw that at the outer edges of the market gardens was the boundary leading to the open spaces used for archery practice. There was a broad ride along the boundary between the gardens and the target ground and some instinct told him to push his barrow that way.

Suddenly, on the other side of the wall, he saw the Magus,

wrapped in his black cloak, with two of his servants setting up an archery target. Other men were already stringing their bows and firing into the padded wheels of the targets.

Jack loaded some earth into his barrow to keep looking busy, and he wheeled it along the outer path so that he could get closer to the Magus, who was standing with his back to him watching the target.

'You there!'

Jack turned, and it was a good thing he did so, for the Magus turned too, and would have spotted Jack. Someone was waving at him to get out of the way, and as he moved himself and his barrow, a proud, tall woman riding side-saddle on a fine bay horse cantered past him. She continued towards the archery targets, where the Magus had clearly seen her.

Is that the woman called the Abbess? Jack wondered to himself. Certainly, by her bearing and the magnificence of her horse, she was no common woman.

A servant held her horse while the Magus helped her down with great courtesy. *She is important and powerful, whoever she is*, thought Jack, *or the Magus would not treat her so.*

The Magus bowed, then he and the tall elegant woman began to walk slowly around the field, talking intently.

Determined to get to the chapel, Jack pushed on and on with his barrow, until he found himself in a lonely part of the market gardens, where frames and barrels and sticks and stakes were kept in piles, along with tools waiting to be mended and heaps of sacking.

He could still hear the thwack-thwack of the target practice over the boundary wall, when he spotted the ruins of the old chapel.

It was not quite ruined, for there was a small stone ante-chapel, roofed and with high windows, and Jack guessed that this must be the place.

Leaving his barrow, and checking that he was alone, Jack cautiously tried the door to the stone chapel. It was locked, but he had his iron tool, and in less than a minute he had opened the door and gone inside, locking it behind him. He looked around. It was not what he had expected.

Inside was an altar, set in the high old Catholic fashion, now outlawed in England since the days of Henry the Eighth, when he had defied the Pope, and made himself Head of the Church of England.

Jack knew that his master, Roger Rover, was a Catholic, and that he had a priest hidden away in the house, and he knew that the penalty for those who followed the old religion was death. But Roger Rover was a favourite of the Queen, and she knew how to overlook what she did not choose to see.

The altar was set for a Mass, but as Jack looked closer, he saw that the candlesticks were made of lead, and that the altar cloth was black, and that there was a strange star on the altar, drawn in gold, like two triangles upside down on one another. *A pentangle*, thought Jack. *This place is being used for magic.*

There was no sign of any of the alchemical apparatus he had expected to find, or that the boys had laboured over in the Dark House. No alembic, no furnace, no jars, no vapours.

It was eerie and empty, waiting, it felt like – but waiting for what?

Jack heard footsteps. He ducked under the altar and held his breath. He could see a pair of feet and two sturdy legs. *Abel Darkwater*, he thought to himself, and he lifted the altar cloth so that he could see more.

Darkwater was rolling a heavy barrel towards the altar. He was breathing heavily at the exertion. Then, he left the barrel and went back outside, leaving the door ajar. Jack peeped out. The barrel was big enough to pickle a man.

What a strange thought to have! said Jack to himself, but Darkwater was returning, and the Magus was with him.

Silver, with Crispis in tow, had followed Mistress Split to a low broken-down collection of sheds and poultry houses, where fowls were clucking up and down, and a few pigs were snouting in the dirt. She could hear a man shouting. Grabbing Crispis by the hand, they crept through a little side door to one of the poultry houses. There was Wedge.

'Hatch it! Hatch it!'

Wedge was standing over a turkey and the turkey was sitting on the coconut. Mother Midnight was tied up in a corner, her black cat lying across her shoulders.

As Mistress Split came in at the door of the shed, Wedge turned and snarled at her, and spat at Max.

'Found your way home like a stupid dog, did you? Speak to the stupid old woman, you disobedient half!'

'You were told she would not speak to you, stupid half

yourself!' said Mistress Split, brandishing her sword at Wedge.

'I want the Egg, Egg, Egg!' yelled Wedge.

'Then Beg, Beg, Beg,' yelled Mistress Split in return.

Mother Midnight laughed. 'Bury it in the ground and then it will split and come forth.'

Wedge looked at her in astonishment. 'In the sods?'

'Get a spade, you clod!' shouted Mistress Split, and Wedge ran outside, dug a hole as deep as despair, and flung the hard-pressed turkey off the coconut, and buried the coconut in the earth faster than anyone could say idiot.

'How long?' demanded Wedge.

Mother Midnight said nothing to him, but grinned her toothy grin at Mistress Split. 'Say to him three days and three nights and he must not leave it.'

'Leave? I won't move to breathe!' exclaimed Wedge. 'Three days and the whole world will be at my foot.'

'And I am made of soot . . .' muttered Mistress Split, hopping off.

Silver saw that with Wedge minding his coconut and Mistress Split out of the way, she had a chance to reach Mother Midnight and untie her.

'Crispis, stay very still! I won't be long.'

Silver ran over to Mother Midnight and began busily untying her hands.

'Jack sent me to rescue you,' said Silver. 'He is at the old Priory.'

'He is in great danger,' said Mother Midnight.

AND TWISTS . . .

'Is everything prepared?' asked the Magus.

'Everything is in order,' replied Abel Darkwater. 'We have only to wait for the sacrifice.'

'I bring news of that,' said a low, pleasant female voice. 'My horsemen have done their work.'

And from under the altar, peeping out, Jack saw the skirts of the Abbess.

While Silver was untying Mother Midnight, Crispis heard horses nearby, and ran to hide himself. There was nowhere to hide at all, except in a field of sunflowers growing on a patch of ground. The men on the horses saw him dive into the patch, and gave chase, but when they came to the sunflowers, it was impossible to tell which was the child and which were the flowers, so, imagining he had given them the slip, the men rode off. Crispis stood very still and upright because he knew that something awful was about to happen, and it did.

Silver and Mother Midnight hurried round the backs of the sheds, where they had no choice but to cross the open spaces of the Spital Field. Silver would have run for it, but Mother Midnight was old, and she was carrying her cat, so as it was they limped slowly along, and Silver hoped that they looked like any other of the London flotsam and jetsam that walked hither and yon – a beggar woman and her boy.

But as they crossed the Spital Field towards the archery butts, where men were practising, the horsemen saw the two of them, three if you count the cat, and galloped up, tall on their horses. Roughly, one pulled Mother Midnight up into the saddle behind him, and the other caught Silver, and sat her in front of him, wedged against the pommel, and wriggling like an eel, but it was no use.

'This must be the boy we are looking for!' said one of the men.

And at that, the horses galloped forward, and in no time at all, Silver found herself tossed to the ground.

'You may release the old woman,' said a voice. It was a woman's voice, and Silver would recognise it anywhere – through the curve of the universe, and all of time.

But no, surely it wasn't possible? Silver looked at the Abbess, who was jewelled and beautiful and perhaps forty years old, but not forty Elizabethan years old, for her skin was strong and clear. She was not a young woman, but she was youthful. Echoing back into Silver's head were the words of Mistress Split, hopping through the Priory tunnels: 'Old is as time does, what is time to her?'

'This is not the boy,' said the Abbess. The horsemen looked at one another. 'There was another, very small, but he escaped us. We shall seek him.'

The Abbess shook her head, watching Silver all the while. 'The other will be nearby. And this one will do very well for

284

my purposes. She is, is she not, *blood most dear*?'

As the Abbess said these words from the Book of the Phoenix, she pulled off Silver's cap, and her girlish hair fell down in its unruly curls. The woman and the girl looked at each other, and it was a long look, with centuries in it.

'Silver . . .' said the Abbess. 'Is it really four hundred years and more since our last meeting?'

And without another word, the Abbess signalled to her men, who clipped Silver to a chain in the wall outside the ruined chapel.

Then the Abbess went inside, and through the open window Silver could hear the voices of the Magus and Abel Darkwater.

She waited. Nothing happened.

Nothing happened. She waited.

Then, with a shiver and a shadow, Silver looked up and saw that the edge of the moon was beginning to pass across the sun.

ECLIPSE OF THE HEART

Jack was still lying like a stone under the altar. He heard the scrape of the tinderbox as the Magus lit the candles, and he could smell a strong incense.

'The quicksilver . . .' said the Magus, 'the Aqua Mercurius.'

'The barrel is prepared for the sacrifice,' said Abel Darkwater, 'and I shall open its mouth.'

Jack could hear him prising the top from the barrel. Then the Abbess came in, with news of the sacrifice, and soon afterwards, to his horror, Jack saw Silver's feet being dragged towards the altar.

'Let me go!' she shouted.

'This is not him,' said the Magus angrily. 'Where is the Radiant Boy?'

The Abbess smiled. 'I promised you a sacrifice, yet I did not say what kind.'

'We had a pact!' said the Magus.

'I want nothing from you,' said the Abbess. 'If I help you it is because I am helping myself.'

Abel Darkwater walked up to Silver. And he walked round and round her as though she were a fish in a bowl.

'The Golden Maiden! The Girl with the Golden Face! Silver! You have many names, but one end, and it is now! We are well met here, for we shall never need meet again – not through continents of history or geographies of time. Do you remember me, Silver?'

'How could she forget Abel Darkwater and his alembics?' said the Abbess.

'I have not forgotten Abel Darkwater,' said Silver, 'and I haven't forgotten you either, Maria Prophetessa, for that is your true name.'

The Abbess inclined her head and said nothing.

'You have betrayed me!' cried the Magus. 'You are in league together, you and this conjuring idiot, Darkwater, and you have both betrayed me!'

'Childish!' said the Abbess. 'Betrayal assumes allegiance, and I have no allegiance to you. You have your sacrifice, and that is necessary for your Work. To destroy the Radiant Boy is a different matter, and no matter of mine.'

'Nor mine,' said Abel Darkwater, 'and this Maiden was ever my price, as well you know.'

'And I have no price, for I cannot be bought,' said the Abbess, in her low and pleasant voice, 'but you mistake me, Magus, if you imagine I have no interests. On this occasion, as far as the girl is concerned, my interests happen to be the same as those of Darkwater. That is all.'

Abel Darkwater picked up Silver against his strong boar-like chest. He seemed to bare his tusks at the Magus. 'You shall get your City of Gold,' he said, 'but when this Maiden is gone I shall soon be Master of Time!'

'The Timekeeper is mine,' yelled Silver, 'now and for ever!'

'Such spirit,' said the Abbess mildly. 'In a strange way I shall be sorry to lose you so much sooner than expected, Silver.'

'And I shall not be sorry!' shouted Abel Darkwater. 'Into the barrel with her!' And he tossed Silver into the air like a fish that is caught.

The chapel was darkening. The Magus strode over to the Abbess, his face close against hers. 'Again, I tell you, we had a pact, you serpent of the Nile! Where is the Boy?'

'He is here,' said Jack.

Jack came out from under the altar. He stood unafraid and still, and there was an authority about him, and a power, that made everyone hesitate.

The chapel was darkening. The moon was halfway across the sun.

'Silver is not to be the sacrifice,' said Jack, 'the sacrifice of *blood most dear*, and neither am I. There is to be no sacrifice. You are defeated, Magus. By my presence here, you are defeated.'

It was a good try, and Jack nearly succeeded. The truth is, he was powerful, but he was untaught, and knew nothing of the magic arts, or what he should do. He simply trusted the power he felt in him, but the Magus was ancient and wily.

'How so, Jack Snap?' he said. 'How so?'

But that was the Dragon's voice. Jack felt a sudden confusion, and he faltered. Who was the Magus? Where was the Dragon? Were they the same? Were they separate? And had not the Dragon told him that any fear or anger or uncertainty would weight the power back to the Magus?

Jack was uncertain. He shifted his gaze. The Magus felt the moment and used it to spring at Jack with claws and teeth, no longer in human form, but some monstrous beast unknown.

In the darkening chapel they fought. The candlesticks on the altar were turned over, the cloth ripped to the floor. Jack saw that as the Magus fought him, his own body was shining like gold, but like living gold, and he lit the darkening chapel as though the sun that was eclipsed outside was bottled inside him.

They rolled and held, and were like creatures welded together; first the Magus had Jack with a claw at his throat, and then by a twist Jack had the Magus locked at the jaw.

But Abel Darkwater had plans of his own. No matter how Silver kicked and struggled she could not free herself. He carried Silver to the barrel of mercury. She was about to cry out, but as she saw Jack in mortal combat, she knew that for his sake she had to hold all her courage in her mouth, for if she distracted him now, even for a second, he would be killed by the hideous clawed beast that was the Magus.

The Abbess stood by. She watched everything. She said nothing.

Abel Darkwater lowered Silver feet-first into the barrel. As the mercury touched her feet, she felt its terrible cold that numbed her legs as she was dipped and dropped deeper and deeper. She was too cold to shiver, and it was as though she had become the cold moon, and the sun had gone out of her. She closed her eyes. The quicksilver covered her. Abel Darkwater closed the barrel.

Without a backward glance he quitted the chapel into the darkening noon, leapt on his horse, that shied at the loss of light, and galloped away.

As the last of the light left the chapel, in the fullness of the eclipse, there was a fearful cracking noise. Jack had the Magus pinned under him, and with his golden strength he saw the half-animal, half-human form begin to diminish and fade. He was utterly concentrated now, and wanted only that this moment should be his, and the Magus defeated for ever.

And then the Abbess said, in her low and pleasant voice, 'Another has sacrificed herself in your place.'

Jack let go.

And his grip on the Magus loosened. And he stood up alone, in the dark, and he was dimmed, and he was lost, and he was nowhere, and he was no one, and he was nothing, scrap, whittle, ounce, speck, atom, dream. The battle was lost, and he had lost, and, and . . .

And the Magus was gone in his phoenix form through the open window.

Jack felt in his own body the emptiness of the universe.

Darkness

Silence

Despair

Jack went over to the barrel, which was freezing cold and covered in icicles. He stood in front of it, hanging his head like a broken beast.

'It is called the Dissolutio,' said the Abbess mildly. 'It is a part of the alchemical process of transformation. Silver, like quicksilver, has dissolved into a million parts. There are millions of Silvers in the barrel, and none at all. Farewell, Jack.'

And the Abbess left the dark chapel.

Jack shouldered the barrel – and it was easy for him to do because of his strength, and he went outside and looked at the sun, and now the eclipse was passing, as the moon sped on, and the sun was beginning to light the earth again.

Heavy in his body like lead, with a heart that was dead as a stone that must feel nothing lest it break, Jack walked, upright and steady, out of the Priory, and down Bishopsgate Street towards the river. His shoulder and arm were frosted and frozen with the frozen frostedness of the barrel.

No one stopped him or challenged him. All the people were dazed by the eclipse, and the strange apparition of the strange boy and his barrel seemed part of the wonders they had seen. And as Jack reached the river, he understood why everyone was amazed, for he reached the river long before he reached the river; the waters had risen and broken their banks, as the Book of the Phoenix had foretold.

Sturgeon and carp gasped in the shallow waters at Leadenhall, and small craft flung out of the Thames by its rising, perched like miniature arks on miniature Ararats, marooned and becalmed as the waters began to recede.

Jack found the rowboat, and rowed slowly and sadly downriver back to London Bridge. The Keeper of the Tides was leaning out of his poop, and he hailed Jack.

'What ho, Jack? What ho?'

But Jack only shook his head and rowed on. He had lost Silver and he had lost Crispis. He had lost his mother. He had lost his fight. He felt that he had lost himself.

At length he reached the water-gate of The Level on the Strand. By now the cold of the barrel had turned the whole boat to white ice. Jack didn't care; he shouldered the barrel once more and took it straight upstairs to Roger Rover's chamber, where he found his old master, and the great alchemist, John Dee.

'I have failed,' he said simply, and two tears fell down his face and on to the floor. He stared at them; they were tiny drops of solid gold.

John Dee bent down and picked them up and put them on the table. 'You are the Radiant Boy,' he said.

'And what of it?' said Jack. 'I have failed.'

John Dee shook his head. 'The Battle of the Sun is not done, my good Jack; it has begun.'

THE CITY OF GOLD

Already it had begun.

'It was my cart and it's my cartwheel!'

'Give that to me, it's mine! Mine had the spoke missing!'

'It's a trick, whatever it is!'

'No! It's solid gold, I tell you!'

The city was changing colour. And texture. And form. And matter. The city was turning into gold.

The first report was when two carters were hauled to the bench for fighting in the street over a cartwheel. But when the magistrate saw the cartwheel, he confiscated it as evidence, and neither the magistrate nor the wheel were ever seen again.

It began with ordinary objects: pokers, tongs, hammers, cups. No longer iron or copper, or forged or blasted – all solid gold.

And the fights – you should have seen the fights. Two people who had been friends for life had each other by the throat over a platter of meat, and not for the meat but for the platter.

A man kicking a stone saw it turn to a golden nugget.

A boy feeding his donkey saw the nosebag switch from coarse weave to shining woven threads of gold.

A woman drying her washing in Fynnesbury Fields found that all her master's linen was stiff as armour and shining in the sun. When she tried to pick it up, she fell down. Half a dozen soldiers made off with it, and she was left with a pair of solid gold stockings; she ran with them all the way home.

Gold. Everywhere gold.

No one slept. Men, women and children prowled the streets with lanterns searching for golden objects, for no one knew when it would happen or what it would be, and you could take a spoon and wish it to be gold and waste your breath, or you could go outside and trip straight over a solid gold ball of horse dung.

The Worshipful Company of Goldsmiths had their best men testing and proving and weighing the matter that came through their doors. It was real gold.

No one went to work. Why mill flour or sweep floors, make clothes, mend saddles, shoe horses, twist iron for carts or plait ropes for ships? Why boil tar or tan leather, why drive cattle, why fish, why water, why sow or plant, why harvest, bake or cook?

If everything were gold, everyone would soon be rich. No need to do a thing!

There was a blacksmith shod a horse and, as he nailed the last shoe, he saw the horse's hoof gleaming. Straight away he pulled off the shoe and left the horse where it stood, and went and sold the horseshoe and took himself to an inn and drank so much that he fell in the Thames and was drowned.

There was a man, and the roof of his house turned to gold overnight while he slept, and he was woken at dawn by the sound of tearing and pulling and banging and shouting, and all his neighbours were on his roof stripping off the gold tiles, and because the man was old, by the time his son came to save him, there was no roof left, so that he was poorer when he woke than when he went to sleep, in spite of his roof being gold, for what is the good of a golden roof if it is no roof at all?

There was a woman rocking her baby in its cradle, and as she rocked and sang a lullaby, the cradle turned to solid gold, so heavy that it fell through the floorboards, the baby with it, and when the mother ran downstairs, she found a mob of men dragging the cradle away, and her babe thrown out and left by the road. She picked up the child and soothed it, and to her the child seemed better than gold, but as she soothed and walked and walked and soothed, a man came by in a black cloak, and he asked her if she was poor, and she replied that she was, and he asked if she would rather be rich, and she said at what cost?

And the man in the cloak laughed and took her baby and held him up to the sun and the baby turned to gold.

Nothing was safe. Nothing was solid. Whatever you had might change its nature at any moment. The whole city was like a gambling den, where men and women waited and watched, betting with their lives and livelihoods that something near them soon would turn to gold.

And while they waited, idle, covetous, what they had

301

rotted and wasted, withered and died.

As objects changed their nature, so did people. Honest men turned into thieves, boys went out in mobs, smashing houses, sinking boats. Women who had been friends all their lives stole from one another, and plotted how to be rich.

At the house on the Strand, all the servants had one by one left to seek their fortune, and so Jack and Roger Rover were left to cook the food and fetch the water for themselves. John Dee had moved himself into the house and was constructing a makeshift laboratory in Roger Rover's study. He warned Jack and Sir Roger not to leave the house in case of attacks from the Magus.

'Didn't you tell me the man was an impostor?' said Roger Rover.

'I was mistaken,' said John Dee. 'And now I must protect us all as well as I am able.'

He was determined to free Silver from the barrel of mercury that stood frozen solid in Roger Rover's study, and not fifty fires could warm it.

Every day Jack went down to where Sir Boris was guarding his mother – still stone but for her golden hair – and when he had talked to his mother a little while, although she could not answer, he asked the huge knight to help with the horses and the heavy work, and the Knight did.

And sometimes, in spite of John Dee's warnings, Jack slipped out, unnoticed, into the teeming stirring bewildering city of lies and gold.

* * *

'Gold! Gold! All gold! Golden turds for sale!'

A woman had discovered that her privy was stacked with golden turds; long ones, fat ones, short ones, clotted ones, some with golden fishbones sticking out the sides.

This trade in turds was so brisk and prosperous that a particular boy, whose turds all proved to be golden, was stuffed with treacle all day long, and his eliminations caught in a golden bucket and at once put up for sale.

Sadly, after a week, the poor child died of a surfeit of treacle and the woman was forced to close her booth.

A neighbour, seeing she had gone, and knowing how stupid people are where money is concerned, took all her own un-golden turds from her un-golden privy pot, and painted them with a mixture of white lead before rolling them in gold leaf. They sold as briskly as before, and the woman left the country before she was caught.

Leaving the country is one thing, leaving a husband behind is another, and he was buried up to his neck in a steaming heap of donkey dung by a furious mob of cheated gold-mongers.

As Jack walked among the restless crowds one day he saw Abel Darkwater haranguing a man at the riverside. The man was driving sheep on to a boat, but Jack could see that these sheep were different – they had golden fleeces.

Jack kept hidden until he had a chance to dart down nearer. As he watched, he saw each sheep, dirty and grey, come out of its pen and pass on to the boat, and as it did so, its fleece turned to gold. Then, as Jack peered closer, he saw the animals themselves breathe their last breath as they became golden replicas of themselves.

Jack remembered the gold fish that the Keeper of the Tides had pulled out of the Thames.

Objects were one thing, but if animals were gold, then soon there would be nothing to eat, and if animals were gold – what about people?

The boat moved out, low in the water, under its heavy cargo. Was Abel Darkwater amassing his treasure, ready to leave London? And what of the Magus?

The Keeper of the Tides had noticed a man in a black cloak standing upright in a dull golden boat. The boat was rowed, oar by oar, by the Creature(s) the Keeper had seen before, and near the Female sat a dejected dog.

As the Keeper watched, the man in black pinned a something of some kind to the pier of London Bridge, and then motioned to his servants to row him away. Swiftly they did so.

'Curious!' said the Keeper of the Tides to himself, and thinking that no one should be pinning something of any kind to his bridge, he decided to investigate.

Jack, pushing his way through the thronged streets of avid faces, was puzzling with himself about the Magus's true intentions. The Magus was only interested in power and in riches, but as the city turned to gold, its citizens were the ones running away with the treasure.

There was something here that Jack didn't understand, and it had something to do with the golden sheep . . .

Jack made his way back to the house on the Strand, where he found John Dee and Roger Rover standing in the courtyard. A woman was with them – Jack didn't know her, but she was carrying a golden baby.

'Jack!' said John Dee. 'Matters are serious and we must speak together. But tell me, have you still those seeds that the Dragon gave you? The ones that rescued you and turned poor Crispis yellow?'

'In my mother's chamber,' replied Jack, his heart sinking as he thought again of poor lost Crispis.

'Then bring them at once!' said John Dee.

Jack ran off, but when he got to the mantelpiece where he had left the three seeds in the cup, he found only two.

'That's odd,' said Jack to himself, but he ran back and gave what he had to John Dee, without saying that one was missing.

'We must plant these, one in each courtyard,' said John Dee, 'and they will give the house more protection than I can offer it, for these seeds contain in them a very ancient magic. If we do not use them, we, like everything else, may turn to gold!'

'My baby!' wailed the woman.

'Wait,' said John Dee. 'Watch!'

And he planted the first sunflower in a patch of earth in the courtyard.

It grew. It grew. It grew. It grew.

When it was perhaps twenty feet tall and thick and strong, it turned its face to the sun and made a gigantic yellow and black fire, as wide across as a cartwheel. As its shadow fell into the courtyard, its shadow was yellow like the sun.

'Stand with your baby in the shadow of the sunflower,' commanded John Dee.

The woman did so, and immediately the baby that had been rigid gold began to soften, and then it began to cry, and then it curled its fists around its mother's hair, and its mother laughed and cried all at once for her baby was more to her than a whole world of gold.

The only change that anyone could see was that the baby had golden hair.

'Remarkable!' said Roger Rover.

'We will now plant the second sunflower in the same way,' said John Dee, 'and all about us will stay as it is – as it should be.'

'I understand why the Magus wants gold,' said Jack, 'but I don't understand why everything has to be gold; every nail, latch, fish and person!'

'Very soon you will understand,' said John Dee. 'By tomorrow morning you will see for yourself why he is doing this. Now this night I must visit the Queen, for the very power of the throne is challenged by the Magus, but first, I believe that I can return Silver to you!'

'But she is dissolved!' said Jack.

'The Dissolutio is not the end of the matter,' said John Dee. 'Come with me and I will show you a great wonder!'

A BARREL OF SILVERS

Jack went with John Dee to Roger Rover's study that had become an alchemist's laboratory. There were the familiar alembics and retorts, and a small furnace burning in the fireplace.

The barrel of mercury had been opened.

Jack looked inside. All he could see was thick liquid silver.

'Observe!' said John Dee, and with a cup he scooped out some of the mercury and poured it into a shallow bowl, where it splintered into a thousand tiny droplets.

Jack looked closely, and to his horror he saw that in each droplet was a miniature Silver.

'There are millions of her!' he cried.

'And none at all,' replied John Dee, 'for while she is dissolved like this she is in a state of potentiality. Do you know what that means, Jack?'

Jack shook his head. John Dee smiled. 'I will train you, Jack, after we have won this Battle of the Sun, and you shall learn what it is to be an alchemist.'

'I am an ordinary boy,' said Jack.

'You are the Radiant Boy, and the power within you is great – yet you, like Silver, are in potential.'

'There aren't millions of me,' objected Jack.

'Are there not? You are young. Are there not many Jacks jostling inside you to see which will become the one Jack, the real Jack?'

Jack went back to look at the Silvers, each in their little ball. John Dee continued. 'Potential comes from the Latin word *potens*, and that means power. To have potential is to have power that is not shaped into something evident and purposeful. To shape a life needs hard work and training – as well as power. In our great art of alchemy, to be in potential is to be ready and to able, yet more than that is needed. Silver must give up her present state of being endless Silvers and become one Silver. She must choose to be who she is.'

'How can that be?' asked Jack in wonder.

'Heat the furnace!' said John Dee. 'I have everything at hand and you must assist me.'

Outside in the courtyard, Roger Rover was haggling with his groom over a jug of water and a pig. The jug of water was a jug of water, and Roger Rover had drawn it himself from the well. The pig was made of solid gold.

'There's no water to be had this side of London Bridge,' said the groom. 'I set off to seek my fortune – heard the streets were paved with gold, and they are. Gold wherever you look – gold, gold, gold, but what are we going to eat and what are we going to drink when the whole place is nothing but gold?'

Roger Rover gave his groom the jug and the man drank the lot in one greedy swallow.

'Fill a barrel,' said Roger Rover, 'and roll it away as you please. But leave the pig.'

The groom touched his forehead, and while he busied himself Roger Rover walked thoughtfully down to the river.

The Thames was still the Thames, as bright and flowing as ever, but a man who drank the Thames would find himself swallowing all manner of infections. The very poor drank from it, but the very poor didn't live long.

'When everything is gold . . .' said Roger Rover to himself, 'yes, everything, every spoon, fork, cobblestone, crate, table and chair, hen and pig, then only what is not gold will have any value.'

''Tis a great evil,' said a voice, from just below, on the river. It was a tall, elegant woman in a rich-worked gown, her face veiled, rowing her own boat, which was strange, and on a river that was nearly empty, which was stranger still.

''Tis a great wonder,' said Roger Rover mildly, on his guard, for he had an apprehension that this might be the woman Jack had spoken of, the former Abbess of the Priory.

'And yet, your own house here seems curiously unaffected,' she said, looking at the sunflowers whose bright heads shone like sentinels over the entire building.

'No doubt my time is coming,' said Roger Rover.

The Abbess nodded her head. 'Time,' she said, 'is more valuable than gold.'

And in that instant Roger Rover knew who she was and where he had seen her before, when the clock that now lay in a thousand pieces in his study was ticking in her hands, in front of the Pope himself in Rome, and this woman had been bargaining for her life.

'Maria Prophetessa!' he said out loud, before he could stop himself.

The woman lifted her veil. Yes, it was she, neither old nor young – *timeless* was the word that filled his mind.

'May I come in?' she said, and tying her boat swiftly to a ring, she held out her hand and Roger Rover had no choice but to take it, and help her up the steps from the water-gate.

Jack had heated the furnace so hot that the room itself seemed to be wavering in the heat. The vapour from the mercury was making him feel dizzy and lightheaded, but John Dee seemed not to notice as he fitted the arms and legs on to what looked like a large wooden doll.

'Pour the barrel of mercury into this mould,' he commanded, 'taking care not to spill even one drop!'

Jack did as he was told, and with his great strength swung the heavy barrel up on his shoulder, and poured the mercury carefully into the open neck of the doll.

'Now we must fasten the head!' said John Dee. 'And when this part is done, if God wills it, Silver will become herself again.'

The head was fastened. Jack sat back on his heels, sweating with the heat and effort. John Dee was saying something in Latin. The room shook.

But nothing happened.

John Dee spoke again, and this time the doll shook.

Then the doll moved.

Then, as Jack watched, the doll's blank face took on Silver's face, and the doll's stiff limbs began to assume the contours of Silver's body.

But then, like those dolls cut out from a folded sheet of paper, not one Silver but seven appeared in the room.

'This is a set-back,' said John Dee.

'What has happened?' asked Jack.

'We have reduced Silver from infinity to seven. But if even one of these seven escapes us, we shall never return Silver to herself.'

'Why would they want to escape?' said Jack.

'Quickly!' cried John Dee, as one of the Silvers tried to climb up the chimney. Jack grabbed her from behind, and as he did so, she squashed down into a ball about the size of the jack in a game of bowls.

'Put her in the alembic!' said John Dee, who had seized a second Silver halfway out of the window.

The other five Silvers were darting about the room. One had got her head through the keyhole when Jack caught her, and another was rolling out under the gap at the bottom of the door. John Dee stamped on her, and she squealed and turned into a ball.

'It is the nature of mercury to behave thus,' said John Dee, 'but it is very inconvenient. Whatever happens we must keep the three Silvers in this room.'

At that moment Roger Rover opened the door from the

outside, and the three Silvers knocked him flat as they raced past him.

'What's this?' said Roger Rover, faintly from the floor.

'What's this?' wondered the Keeper of the Tides, as he scrambled round a pillar supporting the bridge to see just what it was the Magus had attached there. 'How very unlikely! It is a sunflower!'

'What's this?' said Wedge, who had been sleeping and waking and waking and sleeping by the Egg he had buried in the earth as instructed by Mother Midnight. 'WHAT IS THIS?'

Truth to tell, it was a stem and two leaves.

'Power and Glory, Glory and Power!' shouted Wedge to anyone who was listening, which was no one, as he was alone. 'I shall be rich, famous, infamous, Master of the Universe! The Egg is growing!'

The three Silvers were running riot around the house. They knocked over suits of armour, they slid down the banister rails, they swung on the tapestries, they bounced on the beds, and all the time that they were doing these things they shouted, 'Whee! Ha ha!'

It seemed like there was no stopping them as they skidded, slidded, hidded, first upstairs then down, appearing and disappearing so that even Jack who was nimble and fast could hardly keep up.

As he raced past Roger Rover's armoury, he spied a net furled up against the wall, and he suddenly had a good idea. He took the net, got it ready, and hid at the bottom of the stairs.

Soon he heard the 'WHEE! HA HA!' of the three Silvers, and they came tumbling down the stairs like puppies. Quick as a dart, Jack flung his net and caught one of them, squealing and yelping. He squashed her into a ball, and hurried back to put her in the alembic.

'Got one!' he shouted as he came through the door. 'Two left, Master Dee!'

John Dee was in the room with Roger Rover and the Abbess. When Jack saw her, his eyes darkened and he was full of rage.

'Why is she here? She is in league with the Magus!'

'No,' said the Abbess, 'I am not in league with the Magus, nor Abel Darkwater. I help or I hinder according to my own course. That is all.'

'You did this to Silver,' said Jack, holding up the ball.

'Abel Darkwater dissolved Silver in the barrel of mercury,' said the Abbess. 'It seemed to be a solution – so to speak – but it appears that Silver is not so easy to dissolve. I admire her persistence. And I am here on business – to see John Dee.'

Jack looked from one to another. Who could he trust? Roger Rover? John Dee?

John Dee held up his hands in a calming gesture. 'Jack, put that Silver in the alembic. Concentrate on your task. Two of her are left, you say? That is good, and that is bad.'

'Why bad?' said Jack.

'Because of those two, only one Silver is the Silver we want. The other Silver will be her shadow.'

'I'll go and find her – them,' said Jack, and then he looked straight at the Abbess. 'I will not fail, and then you shall answer to her yourself.'

'If you want to be sure of finding the right Silver, you had better use the King's ring,' said the Abbess in her mild and disconcerting manner.

'How do you know about that?' said Jack, his hand going to the sapphire on his finger.

'You are Adam Kadmon,' said the Abbess. 'Jack you may be, but Adam Kadmon is your true name.'

'Jack,' said John Dee gently, 'there is much you do not yet understand about your alchemical nature. All will be shown to you in good time. But now hurry – the quicksilver is unstable, and we must not lose time.'

Jack set off again through the empty house that he knew so well – though peculiar and silent now that the servants were gone. He was worried about Silver, worried about Crispis, worried about his mother, and suddenly he was going past her in the hall, hunting for the Silvers, and there was Sir Boris, standing guard.

'The day is close at hand,' said Sir Boris, suddenly.

316

'What day?' said Jack.

'When you shall summon me for the second time.'

Before Jack could ask any questions of the enigmatic knight, he heard a crashing nearby, and ran off at full pelt, just in time to see the two Silvers disappearing into the armoury.

Jack was after them in no time, but the armoury was full of armour, which was not strange, but what was strange was that the shiny polished suits were like tall mirrors, and in each one the two Silvers multiplied again as they dodged him. As he ran at one with his arms out, he crashed into a breastplate and a helmet; as he ran at another, an empty eerie knight toppled down on him. If it had not been for his great strength, he would have been crushed.

'Silver!' called Jack suddenly. 'Silver, please come back.' He felt that he was being heard, so he tried again.

'Silver, it's Jack and I've come to find you. Here's my hand, here I am.'

There was a shuffle, and the two Silvers came forward, holding hands.

'Which one of us do you want, Jack? Which one?'

'The one that is true,' answered Jack, boldly.

'Tell us which of us that is,' said the two Silvers.

Jack had no idea, and then he heard the voice – the low pleasant voice (*the King's ring* . . .), and he took the ring from his finger and held it out at arm's length. 'The one who can wear the King's ring.'

'The sapphire,' said the Silvers in unison. 'The stone that

is not stone, the stone that is a spirit.'

And as Jack stood holding out the ring, it began to give off a pure white light that flooded the whole armoury so bright that Jack had to shield his eyes with his other arm.

He felt someone take the ring.

'Jack . . .' said Silver.

And there she was, smiling at him with her green eyes, her red hair standing on end like a startled fox.

'Quickly,' said Jack, grabbing the other shrinking Silver just in time. She was rolling away like a marble. He put her in his pocket.

'What was it like in the barrel of mercury?' he said, as they walked back towards Roger Rover's study.

'It was like everything,' said Silver, puzzled, 'all places, all times, all possibilities. I felt like there were millions of me . . .'

'There were,' said Jack. 'I saw them – millions.'

'What happened in the chapel?' asked Silver.

'First, I'd better warn you –' said Jack, but Silver was already opening the study door, and there was the Abbess, and out on the table before her, with its sea-stained bag, was the clock. The Timekeeper.

'Silver . . .' said the Abbess, 'you have returned to us. I am pleased.'

'You are?' said Silver.

'I shall always be pleased to see you,' said the Abbess, and Silver, in spite of everything that had happened, in spite of everything that was going to happen, knew that the Abbess was telling the truth. The most dangerous thing about the

318

Abbess was that she always told the truth. Silver remembered that from the future.

The Abbess turned to John Dee. 'I said I am here on business, and I am. If you wish to defeat the Magus you will need my help, and the price of my help is this clock. In any case, it belongs to me.'

'Don't give it to her!' said Silver.

John Dee was looking troubled. 'The Magus must be defeated.'

'That task is mine!' said Jack. 'You told me so yourself.'

'You have failed twice,' said the Abbess. 'You freely gave him your power . . .' (Jack hung his head), 'and at the second, when you could have taken his power for ever, there in the chapel, you hesitated.'

'Jack!' said Silver, realising now that the Magus was not defeated.

'I wanted to save Silver!' cried Jack to the Abbess.

'And you wanted to save your mother. You are too soft-hearted, and too easily distracted for great power. He will defeat you in the Battle of the Sun.'

John Dee wrung his hands. Roger Rover watched keenly.

'You are clever,' said Silver to the Abbess. 'I remember what you said to me on the Star Road.'

'What? Where? When?' said Roger Rover, bewildered.

'Silver is remembering the future,' said the Abbess. 'We met there. We will meet there again.' And her eyes, sure and glittering like green emeralds, seemed to cut through time itself.

'Madam,' said John Dee, coughing, 'perhaps we might

speak for a moment in private on these matters, and in particular, the matter of the Magus?'

'There is an antechamber . . .' said Roger Rover, and he stood up to show the Abbess and John Dee the way through the hidden door in the panelling. As she swept past Jack, she pick-pocketed the silver ball of mercury.

But she was not the only thief. The second the others turned away, Silver darted over to the table where lay the pieces of the clock called the Timekeeper. She picked up a jewelled hand and put it in her pocket, warning Jack to say and do nothing.

Jack wasn't going to say or do anything. He was feeling miserable and useless. What the Abbess had said about him was true.

Roger Rover returned. 'We shall all be better for something to eat and drink,' he said, trying to be cheerful, 'and as we have no servants, I suggest we go down to the kitchen while we can.'

'What do you mean, while we can?' said Silver.

'There is going to be a food shortage,' said Roger Rover.

In the kitchen, eating roast boar and apple sauce, lettuces and black bread, Roger Rover explained about the groom and the golden pig.

'Worth a King's fortune,' he said, 'but what's that worth to a man who is starving?'

He poured them water. 'And what can money buy for a man who is dying of thirst, except water?'

'So what does the Magus want?' said Silver.

'Power,' said Jack.

'Jack is right,' said Sir Roger. 'The city is in chaos. Men and women have left their homes, neglected their animals, there is no baking done, no milling, no planting, no sowing. And as if food was not short enough – what they have is turning to gold. The Magus will soon control the city, for he is the only one who can turn what is not gold into gold, and, we believe, return what is gold to its former state. He has used men's own greed and turned it against them.'

'And how shall he be defeated?' said Jack. 'I do not know how to defeat him.'

'Perhaps John Dee knows . . .' said Roger Rover.

'John Dee will give the Abbess the clock,' said Silver, but to herself she thought, *not all of the clock, and without the hand it can never tell the time*, and she felt the jewelled hand in her pocket.

And no doubt that is what would have happened, but as is the way with life, something else unforeseen and unexpected happened first.

ABEL DARKWATER

The ship bobbed at anchor at Deptford. It was a rich ship, a ready ship, paid for in easy gold. In Paris, Abel Darkwater had already bought a magnificent house with a laboratory in the basement. In London, he had bought the land to the east of the Priory in the Spital Field. One day, he would build a house there.

He was wealthy. He was his own master now, no John Dee to call him in the middle of the night with some high-minded philosophy about the Soul. Abel Darkwater had more important things to fashion than his Soul; he wanted to be Lord of the Mysteries of the Universe, and to do that, he had to control time itself. And to control time itself, he needed that strange clock called the Timekeeper.

So while others were busying themselves with gold, he had one thing left to find, and he knew exactly where he would find it.

It was easy. The house of Roger Rover was deserted. The groom was in his pay. Together they made their way through the courtyards and up the stairs to the study.

And – such luck, such destiny! There it was, lying on the table for the taking!

Abel Darkwater took it.

Silver felt the jewelled hand of the Timekeeper jump in her pocket. Without saying anything to Roger Rover or Jack, she leapt from the table and ran back upstairs just in time to crash into Abel Darkwater on his way down.

He pushed her out of the way.

'HELP!' shouted Silver. 'THIEVES!'

The door from the antechamber opened and John Dee and the Abbess came out. The Abbess strode to the window, and in a flash, in an instant, John Dee and Silver saw the Abbess rear into a dark serpent, and slide through the window, down the wall and across the courtyard.

But Abel Darkwater had fled.

THE TRUTH ABOUT GOLD

The Magus was at the top of the Dark Tower outside of the city walls. He looked over the higgledy-piggledy roofs and spires of London, some gleaming gold, others casting shadows in the sunlight. The gates out of the city were guarded by the Queen's soldiers. It was as if the city were in the grip of a plague, and none might leave and none might enter.

Food was scarce. Water scarcer. People were drinking from the Thames and falling ill with fevers. At the food auctions, a loaf of bread cost the weight of a baby's head in gold. Where country-dwellers had once tried to enter the city by force to take what they could, and where foreign adventurers had come with weapons to steal and plunder, now everyone whispered that the Devil was in the gold and that London was cursed.

The Magus rejoiced. That night he was to go to Queen Elizabeth herself, and he would offer her unlimited treasure in return for the kingdom – yes, the whole kingdom of England, its lands and dominions. And if she refused, he would continue this siege of gold.

He wrapped his cloak around him and walked down the stone stairs of the Dark Tower. Wedge was waiting, holding his horse. Without a word, the Magus swung up into the saddle and galloped away. Wedge didn't care a fig, or even a coconut, about the Magus, for his Egg was growing.

He hopped back as fast as he could and watered the palm tree, now five feet high.

'I had better find that old witch Mother Midnight!' he said to himself, 'and ask her what to do next!'

But Mother Midnight, after her escape from Wedge and the Abbess, had gone for shelter on London Bridge with the Keeper of the Tides. Soon the two of them – three of them if you count the cat – were joined by Max and Mistress Split, because Mistress Split could no longer abide Wedge and his Egg-work, and she half reasoned to her half-self that if the Keeper of the Tides had rescued her once, he might rescue her again.

In this unlikely role of protector of strange ladies, one dog and one cat, the Keeper of the Tides spent a lot of time fishing, which the cat enjoyed, and she soon found a perch on the window sill, well away from Max, where she could do as all cats like to do; look out and look in at the same time.

It was thus, day by day, that the Keeper of the Tides had noticed the sunflower winding its way across the bridge from the seed that the Magus had nailed there.

It was noticeable too, that the bridge was not at all gold – not any of its houses, shops, persons or animals was in the least bit gold.

'It means something! Bless my maps and globes!' said the Keeper of the Tides. 'But what it is I do not know!'

The Magus rode through Whitechapel towards the Tower of London, where he was to keep his appointment with the Queen.

John Dee was in close counsel with the Queen. Her Barbary parrot preened itself in its golden cage.

'I will not cede sovereignty of England to a magician!' said the Queen.

'You are correct, Glorious Queen,' replied John Dee, 'yet he is very powerful.'

'Fiddlesticks!' said the parrot.

'On what account is this Magus so very powerful?'

'Madam, you have seen the city for yourself! He is the only one who has ever discovered the longed-for secret of turning base metal – indeed any material at all – into gold.'

'And truly it is gold?' said the Queen. 'Or does he keep us under a spell, an illusion?'

'Truly, it is gold.'

'Fiddlesticks!' said the parrot. The Queen laughed and fed it a piece of sugar.

John Dee frowned; he was an important person and not used to being contradicted by parrots. He cleared his throat and continued.

'The Magus has taken the power that was intended for the inner work of the soul and turned it to base use in the world. His power is great because he found a boy, known among alchemists as the Radiant Boy, and one whom we imagined to be a symbol and not a reality. I confess that this boy lodged for some years under my own roof and I was too foolish to recognise him. On his twelfth birthday he came into his power, and was caught by the Magus.'

'Where is this boy?' asked the Queen.

'He is safely at the house of Sir Roger Rover. That house is protected by a powerful charm and is free from the golden plague. This boy has great power, but he does not know how to use it. It remains to be seen whether or not he can defeat the Magus –'

But before John Dee could speak further, there was a flurry among the courtiers, and the Magus was announced.

'Sit by me,' commanded the Queen to John Dee.

The Magus entered like a dark wind. He bowed, but not low enough. He stood up, but too quickly. He called the Queen glorious, magnificent, beyond compare, beyond price, but he meant none of it. The insolence was in his voice.

The Queen narrowed her eyes, and she said, 'There is a bucket in front of you. Turn it into gold!'

And the Magus did so.

The Queen said, 'There is a parrot in that cage. The cage is golden, the parrot is not. Can you turn him so?'

And as the parrot was halfway through saying Fiddlesticks, its beak turned to gold. It raised its wings in astonishment, and they held there, half-flap half-fall, and made of gold leaf.

''Tis a pity,' said the Queen. 'I was fond of the parrot.'

'I can remake him,' said the Magus mildly. 'That is my power. If you wish it, I can turn your whole city into gold, and you will be the golden queen of a golden world, or I can

332

return it to what it was; its filth and chaos.'

'I do not mind filth and chaos,' said the Queen. 'It is life.'

'Choose, Great Queen,' said the Magus. 'Let us rule together, you as the figurehead, and I as the engine that drives the world. You shall have riches beyond the measure of counting. You shall be unassailable. There is nothing that you shall not have for your whim.'

'Except free will,' said the Queen, 'except control of mine own kingdom. Except the choosing of my own life.'

The Magus shrugged and smiled. 'What is free will? What is control? What is life?'

'What do you intend?' said the Queen.

'Men will do anything for gold,' said the Magus. 'They will kill and maim, and lie. There are alchemists, such as John Dee,' (and the Magus made a slight bow, more out of contempt, than in acknowledgement) 'who believe that the self can be transformed into gold – a rare gold, an inner gold, that is of the spirit. But I have shown that men do not wish to turn themselves into rare gold – they would prefer to turn everything around them into common gold that can be spent.'

'Your magic is dark,' said John Dee.

'My magic is the magic men seek,' replied the Magus.

'They do not seek to die of starvation and thirst,' said the Queen.

'That is in your gift to remedy,' said the Magus. 'If you wish it, the golden calves in the fields will be fit to eat by morning. The golden eggs will be ready to boil. The wheat will no longer crack a man's teeth. The fish will dart. The birds will sing.'

'The Queen of England does not make bargains with a street magician,' said the Queen.

The room darkened. The room darkened like an eclipse. The room chilled and the burning fire stilled into standing ice. The courtiers and soldiers began to shiver, and those who could, pulled their cloaks around them. Only the Queen did not shiver, but gazed at the Magus, her eyes steady.

'Very well,' said the Magus. 'Now you will see what power is.'

And he left the palace.

THE SIEGE OF GOLD

No sooner had the Magus departed than John Dee urged the Queen to take a cohort of her servants and friends, and some fighting men, and all the food and drink she could muster, and hurry to the house of Roger Rover.

'It is the safest place in your kingdom, and you must be safe, Great Queen, until the Magus is defeated.'

At once the household began to pack its wares, and carts streamed along the Strand, packed with cheeses and wines, and cakes, and bags of flour and churns of butter. Cows, oxen, poultry were driven through the streets, and many a time the soldiers had to fight off desperate men and women whose pockets were lined with gold, and whose stomachs were empty of food.

The great caravan of the Queen clattered into the courtyards of the house on the Strand, and the Queen herself was soon in the best bedroom looking out on to the river.

'What protects us here?' the Queen asked John Dee.

'The sunflowers,' he answered, 'for they are emblem of the sun, and the sun is emblem of the true gold that is the treasure of the soul, and not of the common gold that spoils the hearts of men.'

'Well said, Sir!' cried Roger Rover, who was in attendance. The Queen laughed.

'But I think that you, Roger, have always had an eye for a certain amount of gold?'

Roger Rover blushed. He had made his fortune as a pirate, and he had made himself respectable by giving a large part of that fortune to the Queen herself.

'There is a balance to be struck,' said John Dee, intervening diplomatically, 'between too much and not enough.'

The Queen was cracking walnuts between her finger and thumb. She was old, but she was strong.

'I wish to meet this fellow,' said the Queen, 'the one you call the Radiant Boy.'

And that is how Jack found himself, dusty and not very clean, kneeling before Queen Elizabeth the First of England.

Truth to tell, she was not very clean herself, for she had not changed her dress for a month. Her brocade was dusty and dabbed with powder to keep the smells down. Over the sweat and the age of her were smells of rose petals and camphor, like an ancient clothes cupboard.

But her jewels shone. And her eyes shone. She was sitting bolt upright by the fire. Her yellow hawk eyes pierced him as he entered, and as he knelt she gave him her hand, crabbed, and veined, and weary and powerful. A hand that had only to raise itself for a head to fall.

'Jack,' she said, and her voice was like a treasure chest, rich and full and sure. 'My advisor John Dee tells me that you have the power to defeat the Magus – but perhaps you do not know how to use that power. I will tell you something. Come close.'

Jack did not dare look up, but he shuffled closer, trying not to breathe in too much of the powdery atmosphere of her. Her voice was low. 'Jack, when I became Queen, as a young woman, I too had power that I hardly knew how to use. And I had to put aside all my doubts, and whatever I might have wanted for myself also.' (And here she paused, and a note of sadness crept in, but in a second it was gone.) 'You must learn what it is to be powerful, Jack, and not be afraid to use it.'

She sat upright again. 'Save my kingdom and ask what you will – lands, houses, honours.'

Jack finally raised his head and looked at the old Queen.

'I will give you all I am made of: my heart, my hopes, my self. If that is enough, I will succeed.'

'The Thames! The Thames!' cried a voice. 'See the Thames!'

Everyone ran to the windows and looked out at the river.

The river's flow was slowing down. The sunset on the water made the water look gold, but that was because it was gold.

A fisherman stood up in his little craft. He took an oar and banged it on the surface of the water. The oar split and broke in two.

The man got out of the boat, and to the great marvel of all those watching, he began to walk across the water.

Others sitting in their milk-boats and poultry-boats, their wherries and sloops, likewise stood up and began to walk upwards, downwards, sideways, anyway they pleased, back to the shores now lined with people.

Jack turned away from the window. Silver was nearby but could not reach the windows for the press of people.

'Silver!' said Jack. 'The Magus has turned the river into gold.'

Jack and Silver left the house on the Strand without saying a word more, and pushed their way through the thronging crowds.

'Give us meat! Give us drink! Meat! Drink!'

The Queen's soldiers were riding through the crowds, trying to keep order, but the numbers of desperate people were swelling the streets. They poured out from their houses and hovels like rats, and they ran to the gates of the city, desperate to escape.

From his Dark Tower the Magus watched and waited.

Jack and Silver skirted the angry crowds and ran to London Bridge, where they saw the strangest sight: the bridge was entirely twined about with sunflowers. It looked as though it were a living thing that had grown like a garden out of the water. Guards patrolled the bridge and would let no one pass, but Jack and Silver slid underneath the wooden piers, and climbed up the sturdy tendrils of a sunflower until they came within sight of the poop-house.

'Hey!' cried Jack. 'Let us in!'

The Keeper of the Tides opened the windows, and pulled Jack and Silver inside. To their great surprise there was Mother Midnight, Mistress Split, and, joy, Max!

Oh, it was a licking and a running and a leaping and a jumping and a tummy in the air and a tail wagging and a barking, racing, braking, spinning, energy dog of delight.

Jack had to lie flat on the floor with the dog stretched over him like a rug, and the dog's nose on his nose, the dog's front paws in his hands.

'That dog loves you,' said Mistress Split gloomily. 'Nobody loves me.'

'Come, come, mistress,' said the Keeper of the Tides, 'I am sure someone loves you.'

'No,' said Mistress Split firmly. 'I am not loved. I know that because I never loved a thing myself until I found that Boojie dog, and then I found it in my heart, my half-heart, to love, and though everything about me is half, my love for that dog is whole.'

Silver felt quite sorry for Mistress Split.

'And because of that,' Mistress Split continued, 'I know that there is such a thing called love, and so I say with certainty that I am not loved.'

And she went and sat in the corner, in the very far corner, with her back to everyone, and with her head in her hands, and she was crying.

Mother Midnight was drinking a flagon of something evil-smelling.

341

'It is my potion of Strength,' she said. 'Silver, you do not need it, for you are of another time. Jack may not drink it, for he must find what he needs in his own heart or not find it at all, but myself and this honourable gentleman must have it – here, sir, drink.'

And with great reluctance, the Keeper of the Tides drank the dreadful brew, while Mother Midnight explained that the Magus had fastened a sunflower seed to the bridge so that the bridge would not be turned to gold.

'He will come here,' she said. 'He has left this place alive for some reason. We are safe here.'

'There is no food or water left in the city,' said Jack. 'And the Magus has challenged the Queen.'

'God spare her!' cried the Keeper of the Tides. 'And God spare me too, for she pays my wages!'

The sun was setting, flashing on the golden river, and burnishing the golden roofs and spires of the city.

'How beautiful it looks,' said Silver.

'But it is not real,' said Jack, and then his face cleared, as if he had understood something. 'The Dragon said to me that when I showed fear or hesitation, I fell into the Magus's power, and he could read my thoughts. If I showed no fear, and if I did not hesitate, then, the Dragon said, I would see everything as it really is – when I jumped in the filthy moat to save the Sunken King I found that the moat was not filthy at all, but like crystal, and clear. The black boiling stink was no more real than this gold is real.'

'Then it is time,' said Silver.

'Time?' said Jack.

'Summon the Knight. Call the Magus.'

'But how do you know it is time?'

'Because you have understood.'

'Yes,' said Jack slowly. 'The Queen is right, I must claim my own power. And now I can.'

'Listen,' said Silver.

And the bells were ringing – across London, from every church, from every tower, the bells were ringing, deep, urgent, as though the stars themselves were clanging through the universe.

And the Knight heard, and the Dragon heard, and Wedge heard, and John Dee heard, and the Queen in her sleep woke up, and the bells rang out across the metallic city, and what hands rang those bells no one knew, but John Dee knew what they meant, and the Magus knew what they meant, and the Magus took his black horse with the golden mane, and rode slowly towards the River Thames.

THE BATTLE OF THE SUN

J ohn Dee had a surprise for Jack when he returned
to the house on the Strand.

Grinning and laughing and eating bread and cheese were
Anselm, and Robert and Peter, and Roderick. Stone no more,
but living boys. William had been freed too, but he had run
away, and no one knew where.

'How did this happen?' cried Jack.

'I hardly know myself,' said John Dee. 'I have been
working day and night to free them, but then, as all the bells
of London began to ring out, wild and clear, the boys
assumed their usual form. But it is about you, Jack, I know
that. You are ready for the Battle.'

'Yes,' said Jack. 'I do not know if my power is greater than
his, or equal to his, but what power I have I will use.'

'Many will help you,' said John Dee. 'You will not stand
alone.'

Jack hugged all the boys in turn, but he had only one
thought, and that was his mother. John Dee shook his head
sadly.

'The Magus has her in a deeper spell than summoning can
break. Win the day, Jack, as you must do, and your mother
will be restored to life.'

Jack went down and touched her face. 'Mother,' he said, 'if I live, so shall you. If I die, we shall be together again.'

Sir Boris had gone.

'Where is the Knight?' asked Jack.

'He is awaiting his enemy,' said John Dee. 'There he is. Behold!'

Jack looked out on to the Thames, deserted of people, littered with boats held fast in the sleeping golden river. The Knight was mounted on his horse in the middle of the flow, or what would have been the flow, and he was still and upright, his hand on the hilt of his sword.

'It is all so still, so silent,' said Jack.

He turned to Silver. 'Where will you be?'

'Nearby,' she said. 'Have no fear, Jack.'

'No fear,' said Jack, smiling. 'I will go out now, and wait for him.'

But as Jack reached the water-gate, there was a tremendous noise in the sky, like thunder, and a flash like lightning, and on wings of leather, and with eyes ancient and glittering, came the Dragon, in one mighty swoop, his voice huge and harsh over the house.

'How now, Jack Snap?'

The Knight was waiting.

And came the Dragon, banking, wheeling, turning, circling, his mouth blowing fire that blistered the banks of the river and ran a black and burnt swathe up the river itself.

And came the Dragon, raging at the Knight, clipping him

close with cruel wings, as the Knight sought to fight him off with his sword.

And came the Dragon, his breath so foul and sulphurous that the people on the bank swooned away from stink and burning. The Dragon's wings were like a pair of leather bellows that flamed his own fire, and when he blew out in a rush of smoke, he fanned the fire he made and sent it shooting across the city, where it caught and burned whatever was left of wood or cloth, and the city that was not caught in gold ran in fire.

The Dragon flew east, and for a time disappeared. Jack ran to Sir Boris, who had been hit twice, and whose armour was damaged. Jack was strong, but the Knight had a supernatural weight to him, and try as he might, Jack could not get him back on to his horse. As Jack looked round, he saw the shadow of the Dragon returning.

But Jack was not alone. There was a huzzah and a hooloo, and right out of nowhere, like angels, like saviours, Anselm, Robert, Peter and Roderick each took a corner of the Knight, and with Jack's help, sprung him back on to his horse.

Sir Boris surged forward, charging with his lance and catching the Dragon in his soft underbelly, at the one open point where dragons can be caught. The Dragon fell.

Men and women rushed from the bank on to the solid river to see this extraordinary sight. The Dragon lay quite still and felled, so much so that some began to climb over him, like a fallen oak.

Sir Boris cantered his horse ahead and raised his sword to

chop off the Dragon's head – but the Dragon was ancient and wily, and with a terrible flick of his scaly tail that flung twenty-one persons from one side of the Thames to the other, the Dragon roared up once more.

And as the Dragon slid backwards, splaying his gnarled feet, it was seen that his weight in the fall – the weight of a cathedral – had opened a chasm in the golden river, and as the Knight cantered forward to deal his final blow, his horse saw the chasm and reared, and the Knight in the weight of his armour had no time to stop himself as he fetched backwards off his horse, and fell down and down and down and down and down into the deep ending of the Thames.

And the Dragon snorted. 'How now, Jack Snap!'

But Jack knew that the Dragon was wounded.

'Go,' said Jack, 'you helped me once. Go and I will not stop you.'

But before any more could be said, Jack heard the unmistakable sound of hooves – metallic hooves on the metallic river. He looked up. Far away, echoing nearer, coming under London Bridge, rode the Magus on his horse that shone like a black sun.

Jack stood up. Everything was quiet but for the coming-closer clip-clop of the hooves.

Jack took the bridle of Sir Boris's horse and leapt lightly into the saddle.

Then, walking the horse around the Dragon, he rode out to the middle of the river, and stood and waited.

* * *

In the house on the Strand, Roger Rover, John Dee and Silver were watching from the open window. The old Queen was sitting upright in a gilded chair.

'I have read about dragons,' she said, 'but I did not think they existed.'

'Everything exists,' said John Dee. 'It is just a matter of finding it.'

The Magus rode alongside Jack and reined in his horse.

'Jack, my Jack, this is all folly. I have defeated you before and I shall defeat you now. Why do you try and fight me? Yet I will offer you a chance. Bow your head to me, kneel before me, and you shall have a share in my treasure and in my power. You shall not be my rival, you shall be like a prince to me. You are too young, you cannot use this unruly power that is in you. Offer it me, and you shall know what power is. I shall soon rule England, and from England, I shall soon rule the world.'

'You will never rule me,' said Jack. 'I would die first.'

The Magus regarded him. 'Die, Jack, would you? Then you shall!'

And the Magus galloped forward, his cloak flying out behind him, and from the streams of his cloak came every kind of evil – came goblins and devils, red-eyed demons and hook-faced birds, came creatures without heads, came heads without bodies, came silent furies and whistling deaths, came claws, beaks, talons, came the tearing, ripping, shearing racket of dark power.

As Jack ducked and swung his sword, Mother Midnight in the poop-house pulled her own cloak around her and flew straight out of the window, calling like a bird of prey, but the birds of prey who came at her call were light and clear and aimed themselves fearlessly at the flapping hells that covered the sky.

As soon as the window was open, the brave little dog Max, seeing his beloved Jack in the thick of the fray, jumped out and landed on fast feet and ran at hounds of hell six times his size.

When Mistress Split saw this, she thought only to save her Boojie, and springing off her one leg, she abseiled down the sunflower, and pulled out her huge sword from beneath her skirts and set to work at every monster that came near her or threatened the dog.

'Slash Mash Crash Bash!' she shouted. 'Come here to be beheaded.' BANG! went a goblin's head. CRASH! went an imp in a cart. MASH! went a pair of evil eight-legged things with beady eyes and nasty fur. SLASH! went her sword, and down went an homunculus with a red face.

'Bless my wig!' cried the Keeper of the Tides. 'Am I to be here helpless while my friends perish?'

And he pushed his ceremonial cannon into the window and began firing cannonballs into the squawking air.

'Take that, and that, and that!' he cried, as a hideous harpy thudded at his feet.

At the house on the Strand Roger Rover took command of the Queen's troops and they poured out on to the river, and never were men braver, their swords flashing, their double-headed axes slashing the sky.

The Queen was on her feet, her lion heart alive with battle. Fearlessly she stood in the fully open window and shouted out, 'The Queen of England is with you!'

And it was time for Silver to do her part.

She ran downstairs and into the armoury and fastened on herself a breastplate and helmet and took a small light sword. Then she went to find Jack.

As soon as she reached the river a thicket of suffocating brown moths covered her face, their wings like stinging nettles. She dropped the visor on her helmet and pushed on, showing no fear at the ghoulish wreckage around her.

Jack was fighting a hellish thing in a cloak that had eight arms and no head.

'Jack! The Magus! Look!' cried Silver.

The Magus had taken his chance in the commotion, and slipped away towards the unguarded house, empty but for the Queen. Jack looked up to see him scaling the wall like a bat.

With one mighty push, Jack shoved his horse right through the swirling cloak with eight arms, and galloped towards the house. As the horse came near, Jack stood up on the saddle like a circus boy, and leapt straight up the wall at the Magus.

The two of them fell, rolling and tumbling over each other.

'Your power is ended,' cried Jack. 'Ended!'

But the Magus struggled free, and ran as swift as a wild

animal through the smoking fighting crowds on the river, Jack pelting behind him.

Before Jack could reach him, the Magus took out a horn, and blew it. The noise was so frightening and eerie that everyone stopped fighting for a moment. Stopped to see what it was that was happening.

The River Thames opened like a wound, and from the deep underground wound came an army of metal men. They had no eyes, no hearts. They walked in step, mechanically, and in unbreakable ranks. The sound of them vibrated on the river. The noise was deafening.

The Magus began to laugh, and his laugh was metal, and his face was metal.

The metal men began to cut down the brave soldiers of the Queen. Lop off their metal heads and their metal bodies fought on. Lop off their metal legs and their metal arms swung their axes. Lop off their metal bodies and their metal legs kicked whatever came near.

Jack watched in panic. *Metal*, he thought. *What can you do with metal?* And then he knew . . .

Jack slipped through the confusion to where the Dragon lay wounded. He sat by the Dragon's head. 'Help me once more,' he said.

'How so, Jack Snap, why might I?' said the Dragon.

'I do not know,' said Jack. 'Melt the metal men.'

The Dragon looked at Jack as though he knew him from a long way off, another time, an older land, and perhaps he did, for there are many things that dragons know. Then, without warning, the Dragon twisted his great head, and as the ranks of metal men came near, the Dragon breathed his fierce fire.

WHOOSH! went the fireball. WHOOSH! went the purple flames. The heat was intense, the heat was as hot as the sun skimming the earth. The heat turned the air into shimmering waves so hot that a woman a mile away had her eyebrows singed off.

The metal men reddened and glowed. Their metal joints swelled and stalled. Their ungiving bodies turned molten, and as they flared and glowed and heated to a thousand degrees, they melted the solid gold of the river where they marched, and the river was turning to molten gold, and the metal men were sinking, clanking, steaming, burning.

The troops and fighters on the river were desperately trying to reach the banks. The battle had become a chaos.

Suddenly the Magus was beside Jack, his face twisted and snarling. 'Save yourself, Jack, if you can!' And with double fury he flung himself at Jack.

As the two fought harder and harder, Jack felt his strength growing, and his mind clearing. He had the Magus by the throat and he was looking into him, through him, it seemed, and what he saw was nothing – emptiness.

'You have no power,' said Jack. 'You are empty.'

A little further away, watching the fight, was the Abbess. She took a little silver ball from her pocket, and held it up to the light. *The false Silver*, she thought. *Let us see what happens if she joins the fray*. The Abbess threw the ball of mercury, and threw it and threw it and threw it on to the river. It rolled and grew.

'It's time to stop, Jack,' said a familiar voice. 'The battle is done.'

Silver was there. Jack looked up at her. 'Didn't I promise to tell you when it was time? Well, now it's time to stop. The battle is over. I promise you. The metal men are defeated. And your mother is waiting in the house.' Silver was smiling. 'Come on, Jack.'

Jack hesitated and let go of the Magus, who lay winded on the golden river. Jack looked at Silver carefully; she didn't smile like that, false and unhappy. Jack said, 'Show me the King's ring.'

And the shadow Silver collapsed back into a ball of mercury and rolled away. The Abbess from her vantage point was displeased. She had expected the Magus to slay Jack at that moment, and while she did not care whether Jack lived or did not, or whether the Magus succeeded or did not, she cared very much to control matters. The presence of Silver, true or false, seemed to spoil that. She wrapped her cloak about her and made her way towards the house.

'Max! Get that ball,' shouted Jack, and the brave dog dodged and tackled between the feet and hooves and claws, and steam and broken iron, and was gone.

As was the Magus.

But now the whole length of the solid gold river was cracking. It was as if a sulphur spring had burst beneath.

Clouds of thick steam rose up. The solid gold was breaking and splitting into little landmasses that were driven with tidal fury down the river that had been pent up. Horses, monsters, griffons, harpies, soldiers, mobsters, fighting boys found themselves on flat rafts of gold, swept away from London and out towards the sea. Eddying and swirling like a tortured serpent, the river returned from its stilled state, and hurtled between the breaking, splintering gold islands, where clung precariously all the old enemies, now crying piteously for their lives.

Jack saw the Magus on a block of gold, using his cloak like a sail, and rafting towards London Bridge.

Jack grabbed a pikestaff from a soldier, and aimed it like a jumping pole to fling himself across the boiling, breaking river, now on to a fragment of gold, now on to an upturned boat, but gaining on the Magus as the tide roared.

'Jack Snap!' cried a familiar voice. It was the Dragon. 'You cannot kill him without his heart!' And the Dragon tossed the Cinnabar Egg to Jack, who caught it lightly, bowing once from his speeding river-run boat, as he and the Magus alone surfed the tidal Thames.

The Keeper of the Tides saw the black figure of the Magus skimming towards him through the chaos of the seething river, and he saw Jack, in fantastic leaps and bounds, not far behind. As the Magus approached, the Keeper of the Tides dropped the net and caught the Magus, spinning him up as a clever spider does a fat black fly.

Now Jack was underneath and, as the Magus struggled in

357

the net, Jack grabbed the net, and such was his strength that the net broke, and the two of them went down into the river. Down, down, down, down, down.

Under the water they were, and the Magus turned into a fish with huge blank eyes, but Jack did not let him go, and the Magus turned into a giant crab, with claws that could wrench a man's arm from its socket, but Jack did not let him go, and the Magus turned into an eel and wrapped himself around Jack's body, but Jack held and held and held, and finally the Magus turned back into himself, and the two of them grappled under the water, until Jack had the Magus's head held back, as he had done with the Sunken King.

And Jack took out the Cinnabar Egg, and holding it above the water line, he cracked it in one hand.

'My heart!' cried the Magus. 'My safe-kept heart.'

And the Magus began to disappear.

'Jack,' he said, bubbles of water coming from his mouth like dreams, 'you were stronger, after all. Ah, Jack, what worlds we could have had . . . what hearts.'

And as Jack held the Magus, he felt something like forked lightning enter him, and he fainted.

What shapes are they up ahead? What sounds?

The river was still under the Bridge. The Keeper of the Tides looked and looked but nothing came to the surface.

Then he heard shouting from the riverbanks, like all of London was shouting from the riverbanks, and he saw that the hard hateful roofs of gold were nothing more than higgledy-piggledy tiles and thatch, and the walls that had gleamed and glistened were plaster and wood again, and the streets that had been paved with gold and shone like mirrors at midday were back to their usual filth and mud.

And across the bank, water flowed into the cisterns, and men and women dunked their heads, and baptised their babies, and dipped their thirsty cattle in the troughs, and the troughs were wood and not gold, and the cattle were warm steaming flesh and not gold, and the ovens were baking real bread, and the alehouses were serving real ale, and all that was chaos and dirt and teeming life was life again and not worth a gold tooth if you sold it, but richer than the universe.

And men and women were hugging each other, and sharing trotters and cabbage, and the city gates were open, and country people crowded in bringing gifts of eggs and cakes, and the soldiers, high on their horses, picked fruit high on the tree, and bent down to give it to the children.

And the fish in the river were fish.

And the birds in the trees were birds.

And the bees were not golden bees, and the flowers were not golden flowers, and the air smelt of herrings and honey-hay, of malt and yeast and pigs, and of the sweet moving day.

And the Queen, in her gilded chair, looking out on to the river, clapped her gnarled and ringed hands.

And the fiddlers played, and the singers sang, and there

was dancing everywhere. And people found that life was better than gold, and that love was worth more than riches. And what had been lost was found.

'Where's Jack?' said Silver.

JACK

S ilver went down to the river, and took a boat, and before she could untie the anchor, Max had jumped in the prow. But Silver had no skill with boats, and the Thames was still boiling in its fury. As she eddied and tossed and made no headway, a fat weight flung itself in beside her and took an oar in its powerful arm; its powerful one arm. It was Mistress Split.

'Row,' she commanded.

Under Mistress Split's direction, and Silver pulling mightily with her two arms, and Mistress Split skilfully rowing her side and managing the unruly tide, Max barking encouragement, the boat passed under London Bridge.

The Keeper of the Tides was leaning out. 'They went down,' he cried, 'and Jack did not come up!'

Silver was full of foreboding, and Max's tail had begun to droop.

'Row!' commanded Mistress Split, and on they rowed, past the crumbling edges of London, and towards the marshes.

And that is where they found him.

Jack was floating on his back with his eyes wide open, watching the clouds. He had no sense of where he was, or who he was, only that he was floating, and that his whole body was tingling like a jellyfish. He did not know it, but he was slightly luminous.

He thought the clouds were cities, and he thought he was dreaming.

A boat pulled alongside him, and one muscled sturdy arm yanked him over the edge.

'You've woken me up,' he said regretfully.

'We're going home,' said Silver.

HOME

W hat a party!
   The whole city of London came to Roger Rover's
house on the Strand.

There were ox roasts and pigs on spits and chickens broil-
ing in stock, and vats of soup, and cauldrons of eels and
cheeses the size of cartwheels rolling through the courtyards,
and apples piled into pyramids greater than anything built in
Egypt. There were tiny cakes to pop in your mouth and cakes
so vast that they had to be sliced with a sword, and there were
jellies with jewels shining inside them, and sugared rabbits,
and sweet almonds.

The dancing had begun, the clodhoppers and the nobles
all together. A lady in silk and furs danced with a cabinet-
maker wearing patched breeches. The girls who carried fish
in baskets on their heads, and whose hair smelled of herrings,
bowed before perfumed lords, and were welcomed that day as
equals.

And equals they were, not because gold had made them
each as rich as the other, but because gold had made them
each as hungry and thirsty as the other. The golden fish on
golden plates were hateful. The golden water in golden
goblets was a torture none could endure.

And those who had hidden fortunes in fields, and went back secretly, guiltily, to dig them up before the party was done, found nothing but mouldy sacking and worms.

The gold was gone.

Jack walked unsteadily from the boat, Silver holding his arm, and Max running beside him. Roger Rover, keen-eyed, saw them coming up through the water-gate, and went down himself to help the boy whose clothes were soaked through.

'Put him by the fire,' commanded Sir Roger, and as the servants began to help him undress, they saw that his body was covered in small cuts and wounds.

There was a knock at the door, and in came Mother Midnight, who had shown her own bravery many times that day. She was carrying a pot of ointment.

'Smear Jack in this,' she said.

It was Silver who rubbed the ointment into his shoulders and chest and on his legs and feet, and as she worked, intent on what she did, she didn't see that each wound worked, healed and closed, and was healthy and whole again.

'Now drink him this,' said Mother Midnight.

Jack drank the steaming foaming brew that Mother Midnight poured from her flask. His weariness left him. He stood up. 'I must find my mother,' he said.

Jack went to the hall where his mother was. Her hair was still made of gold and her body was still made of stone. Jack began to tremble. He had done everything in his power, and he had defeated the Magus, but he had lost his mother.

John Dee was behind him. Jack turned on him. 'You told me that if I defeated the Magus, my mother would be returned to me. But she is stone!'

John Dee shook his head sadly. 'Jack, I do not understand. The Magus is defeated, and his enchantments should fall with him. That is the rule. But, for your mother, I fear that the bond between you was what he hated, the love of a mother for her son, the love of a son for his mother . . .'

'Or father . . .' said Jack, thinking of William, who had run away and not been seen. 'The Magus never loved his own son William.'

'Love or its lack is at the bottom of most things, Jack, as you will discover, though it be covered by a thousand other stories and ten thousand powers.'

'But that does not free my mother,' said Jack, very sad.

John Dee put his hand on Jack's shoulder. 'The Magus bound her with all the hatred that was in his heart – a frozen lake a hundred miles deep in ice is not colder or harder than his heart.'

'But he is defeated!' said Jack stubbornly.

'This dark magic lives after him,' said John Dee. 'Perhaps in time . . .'

Jack shook his head. 'I love her now, not in time.'

Silver came forward. She touched Jack gently on his arm. 'Jack, a long time in the future I have to do something that I have already done – I mean, I came here after I had done it in my world but long before I have done it in your world, but while I was doing what I had to do, a friend of mine got trapped somewhere terrible, and there was nothing that could save him, except . . .' and she whispered something to Jack.

Jack went to his mother and he put his arms around her, and he said, 'The dark magic that holds you fast cannot stand against the love I bear for you.'

Then he bowed his head and stood back.

Nothing happened.

And Jack thought of the Dark House and the stone beds and stone walls, and how nothing in that place felt alive, shunned by the sun, and how it was a dead place, fixed, and hard and heartless, like the City of Gold, and the power of the Magus.

And then Jack thought of the faithful heart of his little dog, and the courage of his friends, and how his mother had risked her life for him, and how a small sad child who nobody loved had loved him enough to rescue him with a sunflower, and how a girl from another time had come because, because . . .

'Because love is as strong as death.'

Jack said it out loud and he said it again, 'Because love is as strong as death.'

And he said it again, 'Because love is as strong as death.'

And the hall lit up as though the sun himself had come to lodge there, and the light was so bright that no one could see, and what no one saw in the white of the light was Anne, Jack's mother, stepping forward on stone feet that softened to skin and bone.

But Jack knew, and blinded by the light, he moved forward with the good instinct of an animal, and he found her, the dear lineaments of her face, the touch of her.

That which was lost is found.

'Mother,' said Jack.

But before anything else could happen, twenty-five courtiers came to find Jack to bring him to the Queen.

'The Queen?' said Jack's mother. 'Here? I haven't cleaned the place for weeks!'

The Queen was sitting in the middle of the courtyard watching the dancing and merriment. Her Barbary parrot sat by her in his cage, preening himself.

As Jack entered the courtyard with his mother, Roger Rover gave the signal, and the trumpeters played a triumphal burst of honour, and every person, without exception, high and low, bowed down, and the Queen herself stretched out her hands in greeting.

'The Queen herself!' said Jack's mother. 'And that is my son!'

Jack went forward and knelt, but the Queen told him to rise and look at her face to face. 'I shall make you a Duke,' she said, 'and you shall have lands and honours for evermore.'

'Great and glorious Queen,' replied Jack, 'many others deserve honour for this day – many helped me. John Dee –'

'Fiddlesticks!' cried the parrot, and the Queen laughed,

and John Dee was cross to be mocked at by a parrot, but it was a royal parrot, and he had to bow his head.

Jack asked that Mother Midnight and the Keeper of the Tides be given pensions, and that Robert, Anselm, Roderick and Peter be taken into the Queen's service.

'And what else?' asked the Queen.

'Can Max have a jewelled collar?' said Jack, and with great merriment the Queen took the jewelled collar from her own throat and bade the dog come forward.

'Kneel!' commanded the Queen, which Max could not manage, but he sat very still, and the Queen fastened the jewelled collar on him and touched his soft shoulder with her sword. 'Rise, Sir Max!' she said.

Max was so astonished that he did not even bark, but wagged his tail so fast that he began to spin around in circles.

And then, in the merriment, terrible sobs were heard, noises of inconsolable wailing, and Jack saw Mistress Split hopping away from the party on her single leg, and he called out, 'WAIT, WAIT!'

She turned, and Jack ran to fetch her, and she was indeed a curious sight with her half-hat on her half-head, and her single arm wiping her single eye of the many many single tears that ran down her leg to the floor and made a half-pool at her foot.

'This lady was in the service of the Magus,' he said.

'Aye, bred by him in a bottle,' sighed Mistress Split. 'A poor start in life for a woman.'

'And yet she served the great cause,' said Jack, 'and fished me out of the Thames too. I would that you give her a small house right on the river, and her own boat that we shall name *Sir Max*, and a licence to breed dogs for your own dear Majesty.'

'So it shall be!' said the Queen. 'Mistress Split-in-Two, you shall breed me spaniels as brave and true as this Max, and he shall be the sire of many a marvellous hound!'

'But he's still my dog,' said Jack quickly.

Mistress Split was so happy that she started to spin around on her one leg nearly as fast as Max wagging his tail, and the two of them fell over and knocked poor John Dee into a trough of apples.

'Master Dee, you shall be recompensed,' said the Queen. 'I shall give you a grand house with a new laboratory for your studies.'

'And that is what I should wish for myself,' said Jack, 'that I should study with John Dee, and learn his arts.'

'It is you, Jack, who is the master,' said John Dee, struggling out of the apples. 'Only you could win the Battle of the Sun.'

'I told you that!' said Silver, popping out of the crowd, looking dirty and dishevelled and wet, and then she said to Jack, 'Jack, you've got to do something about the Dragon. He is asking for you.'

'Is he not dead, then?' said Jack, and Silver shook her head.

'Who is this person?' asked the Queen, staring at Silver.

* * *

Jack and Silver left the crowd and left the Queen and went back down to the river. They took a boat, and at Silver's direction came a little upstream to where a crowd of people were trying to prise the jewels from the leather wings of the dying Dragon. But when they saw Jack they all ran away.

'How so, Jack Snap? How so?' said the Dragon, and his voice was weak and small.

'Are you all that is left of the Magus?' said Jack.

'He had the Egg,' said the Dragon, 'and the Egg contained him, and also it contained me, and also it contained the Phoenix, and also the Knight.'

'Then you are all gone,' said Jack.

'The Magus was sometime a long time ago a Knight Templar,' said the Dragon, 'and every knight is also the dragon he must fight, and every dragon has within him a phoenix. Good and evil are not as simple as the world wishes them to be.'

'Why did you help me?' asked Jack.

'I want to vanish,' said the Dragon, 'and as long as the Magus held me in the Egg, I could only remain.'

'I would like to help you now,' said Jack.

The Dragon moved a little. He was heavy and injured.

'Raise me up, Jack. Raise me up and show me the setting sun.'

And Jack lifted the Dragon as you would a cat, and turned him to face the sun, and the Dragon stood on his scaly feet, unsteady, but he stood, and he plucked a ruby from his leather wings and dropped it delicately into Jack's hand.

'Farewell, Jack.'

The Dragon turned his head backwards so that he was looking down the length of his own body, then he opened his mouth and roared out purple fire, and the fire was so scorching that Jack and Silver had to stand back to mind their eyebrows being burned off, and the Dragon flapped his wings and heated the fire more, and the fire that he made could be seen as far away as Wales.

And when he was all fire it seemed as though the sun himself came to lift the Dragon up, and the river burned red again for the last time, and the Dragon was gone.

It was suddenly evening, and the air was soft and sad. The moon came out. Jack held Silver's hand and they walked without speaking back towards Roger Rover's house, lit gaily with torches and happiness.

'I shall have to be going too,' said Silver.

'How?'

'I don't know.'

TIME

John Dee had prepared his laboratory with great solemnity.

While he roared the mercury in the alembics, and consulted his books, Silver changed into her ordinary clothes, and left her tattered soggy hose and jerkin on the floor. Jack folded the clothes for her, silently, solemnly, then he said, 'Silver?' and from his pocket brought out the two drops of gold that had been made by his tears. 'These are for you.'

Silver took them and she was sad. But John Dee was calling her to stand inside the pentangle. He sprayed magic potions into the air and raised a wind that blew the papers all around the room, but Silver stayed where she was.

'You have nothing of this place with you?' fussed John Dee. 'Nothing – that is most important. Nothing that can hold you here or draw you back.'

Silver shook her head, and closed her fingers around the gold that Jack had given her. It was their secret.

The winds blew, the furnace burned.

Outside, the party went on. Now the courtyard was blazing with lanterns and everyone was dancing. And so no one noticed the tall elegant woman who came by boat and passed through the house like a shadow.

But Max noticed. And stood trying to guard the way to Roger Rover's study.

'The ball, Max,' said the Abbess, quite gently, and although he did not want to do it, Max spat out the tiny ball of silver mercury he had been hiding in his mouth.

The Abbess picked it up, and regarded it. 'This little lost Silver may come in useful one day,' she said to herself and, putting it away, she entered the study.

'I think you need my help,' she said.

This time she made Jack build a fire right in the centre of the room, and it should have burned through the floorboards, but it didn't, and it should have burned the rafters down, but it didn't. And it should have burned everyone and everything to cinders, but . . .

'Cold fire,' said the Abbess. 'The element that lies between worlds.'

'Silver, you must not trust her!' said Jack.

'I have never lied to Silver,' said the Abbess.

'You left me to die on the Star Road!' said Silver.

'That is true,' said the Abbess, 'but I did not lie to you.'

'Where is the Star Road?' asked Jack.

'It is when we meet again,' said Silver, and the Abbess smiled her silent frightening smile.

'When will we meet again?' asked Jack, his throat a big lump of sadness, and Silver couldn't answer, because she didn't want him to see her cry. They both knelt down, the dog between them, and as they stroked him, Jack took Silver's hand.

'Are you going, truly?' he said. And Silver said nothing, but hid her head in the soft black head of the soft black dog.

'Have you any message from the future, that might benefit us?' asked John Dee, and Silver stood up, brave as she always was, and wiped her eye before the tear fell.

'John Dee!' said Silver. 'In 1666 London will be consumed by fire and St Paul's will burn to the ground.'

'I will be an old man by then,' said Jack, 'I will have children and grandchildren.'

Silver went forward, took his hand, pulled him up, and hugged him. 'Goodbye, Jack.'

'It is time,' said the Abbess.

And Silver looked for the last time at the panelled walls of Roger Rover's study, and at the great alchemist John Dee, and at Jack and his dog, but it was the Abbess who held her gaze.

Silver walked into the cold fire.

The flames ate her. Her body disappeared. She felt herself weightless, formless, absent. But she was still Silver. As she passed through the flaming curtain, she was still Silver – many Silvers, many lives of Silver, a piece of time and outside time. She was herself, but that was many. She was herself, but that was one.

*   *   *

In the study, the cold fire vanished as suddenly as it had come. There was no trace of flame except for the faintest scorch mark on the floor.

'She is gone!' said Jack.

'She is elsewhere,' said the Abbess.

Jack went upstairs to his mother's chamber. On the table he saw a little bag with his name on it. Inside was the jewelled hand of the clock called the Timekeeper, and a note from Silver telling Jack to please take this to Tanglewreck, and hide it there.

I sleep in the room at the very top, the one with the bed in the shape of the swan. If you see a ginger cat – it's mine.

The door opened, and in came Anne, Jack's mother. She was worried about Crispis. Where was he?

'He was last seen in the Spital Field,' said Jack.

At that moment there was a terrific banging, like something trying to escape from a box – and it sounded like something trying to escape from a box because it was something trying to escape from a box; it was the Eyebat.

The sewing box that had been simple plain wood had turned golden and black, and a strange golden light shone round it, like a halo. Jack closed the doors and windows, took the poker, and flipped open the lid of the box.

On a rush of wings the Eyebat flew out, but it was no longer the glaring, staring Eyebat of before; it was a large golden and black butterfly, about the size of a soup plate, and with beautiful shimmering wings and gentle eyes. It fluttered impatiently at the window.

'Crispis fed it the Dragon's sunflower seed!' said Jack, suddenly understanding what had happened. 'If we follow it . . .'

And Jack opened the window and the Eyebat flew out, but it didn't fly away, it hovered.

Jack and his mother ran out of the house, faithful Max at their heels. They ran down on to the river and followed the Eyebat all the way to Spital Field. It was dark now, and they could only manage to keep up because of the luminosity of the Eyebat's wings.

At length they came to the field of sunflowers where Crispis had hidden to escape the guards.

But there were hundreds of sunflowers.

Jack and his mother combed the rows, calling, '*Crispis! Crispis!*'

At last, the Eyebat could be seen in the very middle of the field, hovering.

'There he is!' cried Jack.

And there he was, a very small sunflower, quite asleep.

'Crispis . . .' said Jack, shaking the boy.

Crispis opened his eyes.

'It's me, Jack, and it's safe, and we've come to take you home.'

'I haven't got a home,' said Crispis. 'This is my home, among the sunflowers, who don't frighten me.'

'There is nothing to be frightened of,' said Jack's mother.

'You said that before,' said Crispis, 'and look what happened!'

'Well, there's nothing to be frightened of now,' said Jack. 'The Magus has been defeated.'

'I'm going to stay here,' said Crispis, 'I like it here. The other sunflowers are very kind to me, and at night they bend over me to keep me warm.'

'You're a boy, not a sunflower,' said Jack.

'I'd rather be a sunflower,' said Crispis.

All of a sudden Max started barking, barking, barking. He had heard someone; that someone was Wedge.

'Jackster!' shouted Wedge. 'I know you're in there!'

Jack pushed his way through the rows of sunflowers and there was Wedge, accusingly holding a coconut.

'This ain't the Cinnabar Egg!' said Wedge.

'Very true,' answered Jack.

'What is it then?' asked Wedge.

'It is a coconut,' said Jack, 'according to the Dragon.'

'Hundreds of 'em!' said Wedge. 'This way.'

And Jack followed Wedge back round the Priory, and there, growing in the ground, was the tallest coconut palm you ever saw and covered in coconuts.

Jack took one and split it in half and showed Wedge how to drink the milk and eat the lovely white insides. Wedge was impressed by the splitting in half. 'My kind of Edible,' he said, 'and I'm not sharing with HER. Halves all halves but mine all mine!'

'If I were you,' said Jack, 'I'd start selling these. Very rare in London. The only ones. You could make your fortune.'

'Could I?' said Wedge, who was unpleasant but realistic, and knew that a coconut on its own would never make him Master of the Universe, but lots of them could make him rich. 'Wedge's Rare Coconuts . . .'

And Jack left him there, counting them.

Jack made his way back to his mother, who was sitting quietly with Crispis. But try as they might they could not persuade him to go with them, and so every day after that for a long time, Anne walked down to the sunflower field, and sat in the middle with the Eyebat hovering, and she talked to Crispis, and told him stories, and so reminded him that he was a boy, and that sometimes, even when you wished you were a sunflower, it was good to have someone to talk to.

And one day Crispis stretched out his hand, which had almost become a shoot of the sunflower. And the day after, he moved his legs, which had almost fused into a stem. And the day after that, he took Anne's hand, and walked beside her out of the field of sunflowers.

And Crispis came home.

Silver found herself back in the library at Tanglewreck, right by the fireplace. It was night, and the front door was wide open and the night rain was sweeping in. She went to the door and looked out down the bedraggled wind-beaten rain-heavy garden.

'Jack?' she said, but no one was there.

She looked at the long case-clock ticking in the hall, and she saw that only five minutes had passed since she had come downstairs, woken by the banging at the door, and the voice calling her.

No time has passed, she thought to herself, *because I have been outside of time.*

She closed the thick oak front door, and went back upstairs through the sleeping house. The big ginger cat was fast asleep on her bed.

A dream, she thought, *a dream*, though she knew that was not true and it is what people tell themselves when anything happens that can't be explained in the usual way.

She started to get undressed. In her pocket were two gold teardrops.

And Jack and his mother had a fine house on the River Thames and a little farm nearby in Bermondsey. And Jack became apprentice to John Dee, and began to learn what it is to be master of oneself.

'That is the true gold,' said John Dee, 'and the hardest to attain. The inner gold of which we speak cannot be bought and sold or traded in the market place. It is yours and yours alone. And the sun is its emblem. And the battle is fought and lost every day. And sometimes, it is won.'

And Jack took a horse that winter when the snow was falling on the Thames, and he rode wild and long to Cheshire, and through the remote places, and where he had owls and starlings for company, and rabbits and foxes, but nothing of human kind.

And at last he came to the great house called Tanglewreck, and he went into the wide hall, and up the oak staircase, until he came to a small room right under the eaves that no one used. There was a bed there in the shape of a swan.

This is the place, he thought, *this is where Silver is, and now we are in the same place and the only thing that separates us is time.*

And Jack thought about what Silver had told him of her world; how people could fly, and how they could travel great distances so quickly, but none of them could travel through time – at least not on purpose.

Jack sat on the bed. In four hundred years he could see her again, if he just sat here for four hundred years, Silver would come.

'I miss you,' he said, out loud, to no one.

It was nearly dusk, for the days are short in winter. Outside the ground was white. Jack got up and looked out of the window. The setting sun was rich and red, and for a moment everything – the trees, the sundial, the lawns, the hedges – burned red too, their white mantles reflecting the light.

'Jack . . .'

He knew that voice. He turned quickly back into the room. There was no one there, but a ginger cat had come in and fallen asleep on the bed.